Majid Karimi, born in 1979, is

translator, and a university lecturer, who completed his
university studies in English language and literature in 2005. He
began teaching at a university in the same year and after
compiling several textbooks on learning English language, he
turned to literary activities. Some of his works include:

1. *Today's Folks* (A Collection of Short Stories)
2. *Just Around the Corner* (A Collection of Short Stories)
3. *Clockwork Dolls* (A Collection of Short Stories)
4. *Hidden Layers* (A Collection of Short Stories)
5. *The World Behind Glass* (A Collection of Short Stories)
6. *Wounded Thoughts* (A Collection of Short Stories)
7. *Innocent but Guilty* (A Collection of Short Stories)
8. *Flowing Shades* (Novel)
9. *Diorama* (Translation of 50 Great Short Stories from English
to Persian)

Majid Karimi

THE WORLD BEHIND GLASS

A Collection of Short Stories

Illustrated by Ms Armaghan Alimorovat

AUSTIN MACAULEY PUBLISHERS™

LONDON · CAMBRIDGE · NEW YORK · SHARJAH

A CIP catalogue record for this title is available from the British Library.

ISBN 9781398456679 (Paperback)
ISBN 9781398456686 (ePub e-book)

www.austinmacauley.com

First Published 2022
Austin Macauley Publishers Ltd®
1 Canada Square
Canary Wharf
London
E14 5AA

Table of Contents

Preface

The story collection *The World Behind Glass* tries to depict a world that every human being creates in his subconscious and lives in fear. A world that is bigger than he imagined and beyond the world in which he lives. He tries every moment to know himself in the world of his imagination, but every moment, he finds himself in a labyrinth that takes him back to the beginning. Sometimes the path is blocked and it is not possible for him to continue, and this is exactly the time when it creates eerie and frightening conditions for him and frustration and fear pervade his whole being, and every moment man shows a different reaction from what makes his character. Characters have behavioural complexities that through inner monologues, introduce us to what is going on in them and tell us how much each person's past can influence their current life and how it can move forward in a steady stream of consciousness and takes control of him. In this inner world, each person is his own hero and he establishes his own future through his imagination and gives them energy and pursues them. But lack of awareness and faith causes anxiety to take over his whole being and deprives him of relative peace, and over time, as more experiences and hidden layers of his mind are added, his current life becomes more overshadowed. In this world, man goes everywhere and reaches out to destroy the darkness that dominates it, in which not only does he not succeed but it makes him even more frustrated and weak. For this reason, the stories have been tried to be written in a minimalist and short style so that there is more opportunity to depict the worlds of the characters. Stories are a representation of a modern life that the author impartially merely tries to portray and offers no solution at all, because he knows that behavioural complexities are rooted in the characters' experiences and mental reserves that are not easy to access.

Other works by this author include the collection of stories *Today's Folks*, *Just Around the Corner*, *Clockwork Dolls*, *Hidden Layers*, *Innocent But Guilty* and *Wounded Thoughts*, which have many similarities in the stories of these collections. But the main difference between them is the writing style and the creation of story settings that the author has used in each collection and has turned each of them as a completely separate and different collection. Other works by the author include the novel *Flowing Shades*, which interestingly shows behavioural instabilities as a stream of consciousness. It should be noted that the collection of the story *Clockwork Dolls* has also been published by Austin Macaulay Publisher in London with the author's own translation and has been distributed in the United States, Canada and other European countries. The collection is also donated to the Dublin, Oxford, Cambridge and Edinburgh libraries.

This collection is written for the general public and those who are interested in literature, short stories and art, and I hope they enjoy reading it and follow the other fiction collections mentioned.

In the end, I need to thank the management of Austin Macauley Publishers and their colleagues for their compassionate cooperation to publish my works.

Majid Karimi

Grey Pavement

Grey Pavement

For the several times, he went to his closet and took out his birthday necklace, which he had been given as a gift last week, and dropped it around his neck. He could not understand the connection between this necklace and his mental state. Perhaps when he opened the gift, he did not pay much attention to it and did not think at all that a simple necklace could engage his mind during the week. He was sure that this necklace is not only unusual but that it must have a message that he has been waiting for it for years, because he felt it with all his being. The issue seemed more complicated than he thought. He looked at it more carefully so that he might find the secrets in it. It was a leather string with a silver medal on it and had a special design. Surely, its beautiful design could not have so much occupied and disturbed his mind. But because he liked it so much, it made him think. Although he had no particular attachment, he was always fascinated by such ornaments, regardless of their material value. At least, he could not pretend that it did not catch his eyes. He went to the mirror to look at it more dominantly so that he might discover its inner secret. When he reached in front of the mirror, he could hear his heart beating. As if the magical power of the necklace in the mirror has doubled. He could not even control himself. He had been in very difficult situations during his life, but he had never experienced such a feeling. He remembered the hard times of his life, during which he had never rested and had always faced a lot of chases and escapes. Even now, looking at his face, he did not have the freshness and youth of his past, and he looked much older than a person in his thirties. Although those around him always told him that his face had a certain maturity, he knew that maybe there was some kind of compliment in their conversations and that at least he was honest with himself and knew that the reason, in addition to maturity and experience, was a kind of aging, has happened to him during this period. He had set out on a path in life that ultimately meant nothing but what he was now, and it was impossible to explain to the few people who played the role of friends in his life. He sometimes even thought that he had inadvertently entered a lifestyle that resulted in the same situation he is currently in. A kind of depression and loneliness along with the frustrations of lost days and years, had isolated him, and he had progressed to the point where he thought he was used to the situation and had no desire to change it at all. He felt so rejected that the best way to continue was to remain silent. Perhaps if he had not seen these few friends, whom he met only every year at his birth, he would have come to believe that he is the only person living on the planet. Even when he was in his apartment on weekends, he would talk to himself a little loudly to feel someone by his side.

He put his hand on his face and stroked his long, brown, irregularly tangled beard. He had been in this form for several years and thought that by shaving his beard he could reduce his age a little. But looking again, he soon realised that he was used to it. He picked up the medal hanging around his neck again and turned it upside down in front of the mirror. Meanwhile, his eyes fell on a wound on one of his hands. It was a good souvenir for his stressful days, which showed it with a double and prominent posture on his exercised body and muscles. He thought more. He felt that there must be a connection between his mood and the wound on his hand and the gift he wore around his neck and his appearance. And for the first time, he came to the conclusion that he had seen this necklace before, and perhaps that is why it is so special, and in fact, this is why he is upset and intends to find the missing link in his mind. He tried to focus more. He probably had a good result. He re-examined the puzzle pieces together. There was definitely a reason because he was so sensitive.

Why should the scar on his hand created a few years ago, be new to him now? He looked at his face and appearance. Even the way he dressed was interesting to him. He was wearing grey jeans, which showed that his body and limb were twice as fit. But what was most interesting to him was the feeling that assured him, he was standing exactly where he seemed to have seen everything before. Suddenly, his suspicion turned to certainty. Involuntarily, he went to his bedroom and started searching inside the closet with great excitement. He soon pulled out all the contents of the closet but could not find what he was looking for. He was not disappointed at all and continued his search with more determination. It had been a while since the necklace he had received as a gift had changed his mood. He had to find a good reason for his condition. He went to the shelves of his library. But it was useless. He remembered a box in which he put all his extra belongings, which were important to him. He immediately pulled it out from under the bed and opened it. Inside, in addition to a few leather bracelets and a number of rings, was a bunch of paper, several of which were tubed. He took out of the box the tubular papers that looked quite old and that the dust had affected their quality for years; like someone who does not have the courage to do something, he stopped working. There was a light in his eyes that seemed to have answered his questions, but it was as if he did not dare to open them and unveil the secrets. He sat on the edge of the bed and remained motionless. He looked at the room from the corner he was sitting. Everything looked as he had imagined. Next to the bed was a small table with a lampshade, and next to it was a bible showing off its red leather cover. He used to read a few pages of it regularly before going to bed, and he believed that this would bring him some peace of mind. In front of it was a small library that filled his lonely time. On the other side of the room was a simple chair and desk with a reading lamp on it, and next to it was a street-facing window that he often stood in front of it, watching people move around. He got up and went to the desk. He turned on the reading lamp, pulled out a chair, sat down on it and then laid the papers on the table. He took a deep breath and carefully opened the string that was tied around them, and in disbelief, he saw before his eyes the memories of fifteen years ago when he was once drawing and painting. He could not believe how he had changed so much during this time and how he had turned from such an artist to such tendencies. He recalled a time when he sat in front of a painting tripod for hours, applying all his imagination to the canvas and how he had drawn his creative mind in a direction where nothing but loneliness and anxiety could be found. The beautiful scenery he had created in his youth was so fascinating that each one could take him back to his first place. The colours were each so artistically blended that if he did not know he was the creator, he could say that they are perhaps the best works he has ever seen. He looked at the scenes one after the other and subconsciously wondered why he had not even framed one of them and hung it on the wall in his room. Not even one of his friends knew that he had the ability to bring his imagination to the real world and expose it. Perhaps if he had introduced his artistic ability to them, he would never have been accused of having no feelings, living alone in his apartment without any sincere connection, and paying no attention to anything but his work, what made him a violent and determined person and showed a serious face in front of his friends. Even he himself believed that they were right, and now that he saw his artistic drawings and paintings in front of himself, he was in confused. He could not believe that it was he who had been doing art for a long time. But suddenly, he remembered and thought that he was looking for something else. Although he was fascinated by these things, he knew that he had to find what he was looking for in these papers. He turned the pages faster. Most of them were scenes painted with watercolours and oil paints. But among them came a painting that he was actually looking for. The only painting that was drawn with a black pencil and used the art of light shadow. He took it out of the other papers. He then bent the reading lamp over it to provide more light and to be able to see well and not lose details. Fear pervaded his whole being. He could not believe it. He stared at them for a moment without moving. He could not move. He saw a man standing in front of him, on a piece of paper by the window, leaning on it, and that man was exactly him today. It was unbelievable that he designed his appearance fifteen years ago to be exactly what he was today. He wore grey jeans and a necklace with a medal around his neck. His body as it was painted was fit and trained, and to his amazement, he had scars on his hand that he had never had on his body at that time. His body trembled when he saw tattoos on his left shoulder that he did not think had anything to do with it. Even the tattoo design was the same as what he had on his shoulder now. He hurriedly checked the other details. Hopefully, he may have deluded and misunderstood in his imaginations. It was very difficult for him to justify them, and he preferred to consider them accidental in order to alleviate the emotional pressure on him at that moment. But the design, which was barely visible on the medal, was also close to the design of the necklace around his neck. He paid attention to the space in which he was. It was almost obvious that he had simply designed the space he had been living in for several years. The same library and bed, with the same simple study desk that the designer depicted them with great care at the entrance. On the bedside table were exactly what was in the painting, bedside lamp and a small, thick book next to it. He stared at his own image again. His long beard caught his eyes. He recalled that when he painted this painting, he was in a completely different situation from what he was now. He did not even have a beard on his face at that time, and how cruelly he had painted his future face so tired and broken. It was more like a nightmare than a painting. It was as if he had architected his future well and mapped it out on paper, and in those fifteen years, he had followed the same path that his youthful mental imagery had shown on paper. Tears welled up in the corners of his eyes. His heart wanted to go back in time and teach his young ruthless mind how he had played with his body over the years and how, with all his cruelty, he had suffered a fate that he could not get rid of at the moment. He wondered why, when he could portray him cheerfully and successfully, he had made him so tired and helpless and alone, and he had laid the foundations of his architecture so sadly. He even thought about what he was thinking when he painted the scars on his hand and why he included it in his painting. He could even portray the kind face and make him happy and free from sorrow. Why was he really his hero that he painted at a young age? Perhaps from the very beginning, a ruthless face penetrated his being, which left such an image of unkindness. He tried to find more details and decode. Fear gripped him even more when he feared that there were still points in the painting that would come to him in the near future. He even wondered if he had painted any other pictures of himself that he would soon encounter. Anxiously, he turned over all the papers in front of himself. He tried to concentrate and remember whether that was the case. Tears flowed from his eyes. Even if there was a painting, he did not keep them. The relocation of the apartment in these few years had caused him to either donate or sell many of his belongings. He threw away the rest and came to this apartment with a small amount of equipment that covered a simple life. There were certainly other paintings, but he could not remember if he had kept them and if so, where he had placed them. He was completely agitated and restless. He still saw a lot of unspoken in the painting and this made him more worried. He did not want those unspoken things to happen and to live in such conditions. He was willing to do his best to improve the situation. But when he remembered that his present condition was due to the ideas he had developed in his youth and that he himself was his architect, he became more frustrated and blamed himself. He could be better off now and no longer need to spend his life in isolation.

Suddenly, his eyes flashed. It was as if he had found a way to get rid of the spell he had created. It certainly could have been effective. He tried to provide what he sees in the picture and to be exactly as he created it. So he got up in a hurry and tried to make the room look like the one in the picture. Then he looked at his own appearance. In addition to jeans, he wore boots he had bought similar to last year. He took them out of the closet and put them on. Then he had a metal watch in one hand and a leather bracelet in the other, which he held as he saw it. Everything else was exactly as it had been. Just next to the window was an empty vase that had a strange shape. There was no such vase in his apartment. But in the living room, there was a vase that looked a bit like it. He brought it quickly and put it in its place according to the plan. He had almost executed the plan well and had made his dream come true. By doing so, he wanted to put an end to this issue, and this time consciously take a step to paint a beautiful picture of the future of his next days, in which sorrow and depression, violence and anxiety have no way out. He placed the paper on the table so that he could dominate it and see it well to match his standing position in the painting. He stood behind the window like a painting and leaned on it. Then he raised one of his legs and turned his head outward in a special way so that he could see the street and the movement of people. The drizzle had soaked the streets and sidewalks, and the cloud covered the sky and doubled the autumn sunset, and as he looked at the grey pavement of the street and the sidewalk, he thought about drawing a painting in which the colours would wave and the joy would be in the whole existence of his paintings, and he would no longer be alone and his face would be full of energy and motivation, and he would know exactly what he wants from his future. Then, when it is finished, replace it with a painting he drew fifteen years ago and embody a dream that he will not regret after it comes true.

Labyrinths

Labyrinths[*]

The snowfall had made the trail slippery, making it difficult to climb the remaining few metres. Perhaps he never thought he would have to climb such a high mountain and find himself on the verge of climbing. This was a good incentive to continue, due to the dangers of the route and the difficulty of the way, although he seemed completely inexperienced to do so. A thick fog covered the heights, and as far as the eye could see, it was only white, which, along with the snow, had exhausted the eyes. The cold and fatigue of the journey had crippled his legs and he no longer had any focus or control over them. His hands, completely immersed in the

---

Labyrinth: According to Greek mythology, the labyrinth was the name of a structure built by the legendary Greek craftsman Daedalus at the behest of King Minos, king of Crete. Minos' purpose in building such a structure was to trap another mythical creature with a cow's head and human body, called the Minotaur. Labyrinth has a magical architecture and all the drawings drawn from it do not end anywhere.

gloves, no longer listened to him. A cold sweat had taken over his whole being, and with each passing moment, he lost the ability to continue. Although he could understand all these conditions, he did not really feel anything. Violence was the only thing that filled the whole environment. However, this violence in the form of the beauty of nature was so ironic that no one could recognise it. There was only one way to overcome the crisis and that was to continue and cross a path that now sees nothing but the whiteness of snow and foggy weather. He looked around, not even seeing the footprints he had left a moment earlier. The anxiety had taken over his whole being, and it reached its peak when he looked at himself to examine his condition. In disbelief, he realised that his whole body was covered in snow and that he had become like a snowman who remained motionless. The fear of heights that was always with him added to this concern, so that he suddenly found himself on the verge of falling. In order to be able to control himself and prove that he can move, he raised one of his legs. But suddenly, a kind of weightlessness took over his whole being and he was suspended between the sky and the earth with great speed, and he fell quickly without being able to maintain his balance. He could not even breathe in terror. His eyes were closed. He was desperately trying to grab something and prevent it from falling and being destroyed. His heart was pounding at every moment, and he was spinning in the sky looking for a way to escape, but he knew he did not have much time. So he gathered all his strength and shouted loudly, "Help, help!"

He came to his senses suddenly with the sound of his shout. It was as if someone had heard his voice and come to his aid. He opened his eyes. He looked around slowly. Frightened, he found himself inside a tent that surrounded him in the dark. He no longer threatened to fall. Whatever it was, it was just a cold and a nightmare that had troubled his mind over and over again and he could not find a way to get rid of it. Disappointed with the repetition of these nightmares, he recovered and a satisfied smile settled on his lips. He had come there for this purpose. This was exactly the new version that the psychoanalyst had prescribed for him and encouraged him to face these repetitive nightmares. It seemed like hard work. Perhaps now that science was so advanced, he expected an easier way to get rid of these nightmares. He had tried many times to forget them. Sometimes he convinced himself that he might not have seen anything at all. But every time he approached the night, he expected it to call him to the snow-capped heights again. But the fear of falling convinced him to seek better treatment.

Even having fun during the day could not reduce his night-time restlessness or he could not remember exactly when he had this problem. All he knew was that a lot of time had passed. He made his final decision when he left the psychoanalyst's office and promised himself that he would do what the psychoanalyst had suggested. Maybe he was right, if he could overcome his fears once, he could save himself forever. But the same decision seemed just as frightening as the free fall. It was not easy for someone who is afraid of loneliness and falling to see the foggy and snowy path of the heights. Even the thought of it could be annoying. But when he thought about his nightmares, he found no choice but to overcome his fears.

The air inside the tent was moderate to the cold outside, but it was time to get out of the tent and drink some hot drinks. He opened the tent. It was morning. The sunlight that shines on the white-covered slopes of the heights is reflected and strikes his eyes with multiplied intensity. He quickly put on his sunglasses to prevent injury. He felt weak and tired, but he knew very well why. In his sleep, he had expended so much energy that he could scream. He even knew the cause of his back muscle fatigue. The walks of these few days and the night struggles that sometimes came when asking for help added to these fatigue. Although his attitude towards what he wanted to do changed every moment, he could not forget his final decision.

Sometimes he was so frustrated and worried about what he wanted to do that he questioned all his struggles, and sometimes he felt so energetic that he would eliminate the cause of his insomnia as soon as possible so that he could feel a lot of energy. But these momentary changes caused him to become worn out, and he loved to climb to the heights to eliminate the source of this fear, enlighten the dark spots of his mind and be saved. When he thought about these issues, he found himself inside labyrinths that open a new path for him every moment and block another path in front of him every time. Perhaps the reason for all his social frustrations and anxious depressions was rooted in the same labyrinths that surrounded him and instilled in him a kind of uncertainty. He thought to himself that every time he entered the labyrinths, he would find himself in a place completely unfamiliar to him, and after a short time, he would find himself on the threshold of the path from which he had begun. This multiplied his current anxiety and horror, and sometimes more determinedly, to find a solution again and end it. He started again and experienced a new path that again caught him in the same trap and created a state of instability in him. A repetitive turn that he could not comprehend. But this time, he seemed more equipped and determined. It is as if he provided a road map to climb to the heights and from there he looked around and had a look at everything. When he put the psychoanalyst's words together in this regard, he felt that he fully understood the taste of his words and did not need to justify or resist what had been advised to him. He had gained so much experience in this field that he became like an expert who knew the way well at a glance. The only problem he felt was a little courage and bravery so that he could deal rationally with his fears and avoid despair.

He came out of the tent, first looking at his watch and then at the sky to make sure the atmosphere was right for his ascent. Anyway, he was on the verge of climbing and his last home. It took him a few days to reach the main slope and prepared for the final climb. He opened his backpack, poured some of the cold drink into his glass, and then examined some of the food he had left. To climb, it was essential to have the necessary strength. So he took out the can and opened it and began to eat. It was as if he was just getting the supplies he needed a few days ago. He had no experience in mountaineering, so he spent some time studying and gathering information. He made a list of things that might be needed in such a situation and carefully packed them in the same bags he had in front of him. When he told his co-workers about the climb, they were all shocked and thought that he might be insane or that he intended to use this trick to justify the manager to approve his leave. But for them, it was considered suicide. Especially for someone who is getting older and his retirement years are near. Maybe it would have been better to wait a little longer and step on this dangerous climb after retiring. But he was not able to see the restlessness of the night, seemed to be reason enough to embark on this dangerous experience. When he realised that he should not tell his friends and colleagues about his decision, almost all of them found out about it and accused him of some kind of madness. But he loved this madness, because he felt that at least once in his life he cared about himself and did something that, according to the psychoanalyst, could bring him peace of mind. But what if he misunderstood what the psychoanalyst had told him? Perhaps the psychoanalyst did not mean to climb and ascend to the heights of what had come to his mind. Maybe it was just his intention to overcome his fears and get rid of his anxiety. However, it was not logical that a psychoanalyst persuaded him to do something dangerous. But perhaps it was he who wanted to know what was going on at the heights he occasionally climbed in his nightmares. Excessive curiosity had emboldened him to take such a dangerous step. So when he asked his manager for leave, he said he was going on a vacation because the psychoanalyst had offered him one. The manager, who had heard from others about his ascent to the heights, was surprised and asked about it. To end the discussion, he smiled and said that these were just jokes that his colleagues had made with him, otherwise he would not have the right conditions or experience enough to do so. He only needs a few days to rest by the beach. The manager, who was fully aware of his smile, trusted his words and approved of his leave. The only problem that delayed this ascent was studying and gathering enough information and on the other hand finding heights that seemed both easier to climb and similar to what he saw in his nightmares and falls. This part of the job seemed a bit difficult. Because it was almost impossible to find heights that were full of snow and covered with fog and on the other hand did not endanger his life by climbing it. In addition, not having enough experience made the risk more tangible. So he spent time on the outskirts of the city to find such an area, until he finally found the space where he was now sitting and eating canned beans. He had even travelled several times to practise on a variety of routes, gathering information from locals and professional mountaineers who have active pages on official websites. It seemed that all the preliminaries of this matter have been foreseen and it was not permissible to wait any more, and this long delay was the same fear that the psychoanalyst has mentioned many times. Fortunately, he was still feeling the vivacity of youth in his body, and this had reduced the stress and pressure of climbing a bit. Although many climbers had different opinions about these heights, but in general, all of them considered this route to be the best and easiest route for those who are completely unprofessional and have just started to climb. But none of them were aware of his fear of heights. Maybe if he told them that he had a problem with height from childhood or that he was going to climb alone, they would all warn him that it was dangerous. It was as if he was just seeking confirmation, so he did not cite any information that would dissuade him from doing so, and this stemmed precisely from the experience of telling the truth to his colleagues, which was a good experience for him instead, and in fact, on the same day, he decided to simply provide information to others to further his goals. The only thing left was that someone should finally be informed of his decision, so that they could come to his aid if something happened. He had found a solution for this issue as well. In a letter to one of his colleagues, he wrote down the address and everything he needed to know, sealed it and gave it to him, asking him to open it after seven days. During his studies, the whole ascent took three days, and the return route took two days, for a total of five days. So when he returned, he had enough time to tell his colleague before the envelope was opened that there was nothing to worry about. Perhaps this was the first time he had moved so resolutely towards his goal and decision and was not afraid of anything. He was not even afraid to reach the usual labyrinths on his way and bring him back to the beginning of the path he had started a few days later.

He put all his belongings in his bag and gathered his tent. It seemed that he did not act too unprofessionally and during these two days he did well and went according to plan. The only problem with this height was that it instilled in him a moment of excitement from the fear of heights. But he was quite happy to look around, for he had so far dared to set foot on a path he had never been able to see. The atmosphere was exactly like the nightmares he was experiencing. He could hear the sound of his footsteps on the snow. He tried not to look behind him to overcome his fear of heights. As it passed and moved upward, the snow on the trail grew deeper and deeper, increasing the amount of fog. The wind also spun snowflakes in the air, making it harder to cross. On the verge of ascending, he thought that after reaching the highest point, there would be no more falls and he would experience a new opportunity in life. He gradually remembered the words of the psychoanalyst who had promised him new circumstances. Maybe this time, he could go through the labyrinths of his life and find out what awaits him after climbing the heights. Something that was more like a dream for him. He plunged his tired legs harder into the snow to prevent him from falling. He spent some time like this. He stopped for a moment. He raised his head to measure the remaining path. It was foggy and snow-white everywhere, making his eyes dim and unable to see beyond. He estimated the route taken. He was sure that there were no more metres left above the heights. He had to keep going. A cold sweat filled his whole body. His legs were completely paralysed and he could no longer feel cold or tired. His hands were frozen inside the gloves and he had no focus or control over his limbs. As he passed, he lost the ability to continue. He knew he had to move, but he could not keep his balance. Perhaps he should not have stopped at all, and his stopping had caused hesitation to shake his heart and raise his heart rate. He looked around. The beautiful nature portrayed unparalleled violence for him. He looked at himself. He saw nothing but the whiteness of the snow. He was sure he had seen these pictures before. Maybe it was the images he was pursuing in his nightmares. Everything went according to plan. But the fear of the end he saw in the nightmares did not leave him for a moment. He looked behind himself. He was convinced. There was not even a trace of his footprints left. Worry took over his whole being. He remained motionless like a snowman. He found himself on the verge of falling.

He should not have doubted. At the very moment when he had doubts in his heart, all his plans destroyed. He was confused. In order to control himself and get rid of his doubts, he tried to overcome this state by moving forward. Suddenly, he felt weightless and found himself suspended in an empty space. He no longer felt anything. Whatever it was, it was fear that filled his whole being and pressed his eyes tightly together. He gathered all his energy. There was only one way left. He must shout and ask for help. Maybe someone hears his voice. "Help, help!" he shouted loudly.

Suddenly, he felt calm. He opened his eyes immediately. It was as if someone had heard his voice and come to his aid. He should have shouted sooner. He found himself lying on the bed in his apartment, threatened by nothing but his nightmares. This nightmare was familiar to him. He had seen it again and again. There was no problem. He rolled his eyes to make sure there was no fall. He looked at his watch. It was time to leave. He got up and sat on the bed, looking at the backpack he had prepared the night before to climb the heights.

He smiled bitterly. He did not understand the necessity of climbing. The number of nightmares of falling from the heights had risen, as if standing at the beginning of another labyrinth.

Tamimah

Tamimah[*]

The autumn wind blew through the garden trees and shook their naked bodies with them. Coloured leaves also danced in the wind and scattered to each side. The clouds covered the sky and darkness was everywhere, so that I did not seem to be at the beginning of the day. The coldness of the air could be felt from inside the old villa. Although the heat of the fireplace prevailed over the cold outside, the eye could still feel the cold behind the window glass. I had been standing in front of the window with my hands on my chest for a while, looking out at the view. If I had this scene in front of me on a normal day, I could boldly say that it was the most beautiful painting ever created. The fusion of colours and the caress of the autumn wind, which gently showed the change of seasons, and the intertwined clouds, which at every moment

---

[*]***Tamimah***: *It is a combination of a bracelet and a ring, usually with decorative chains on the hand, which attach the ring to the bracelet. We have to say that Tamimah is one of the elements of popular culture and in the past, it was not just a decorative aspect and they believed in its transcendental effects.*

tended to rain, were each a reflection of the absolute beauty of the painting, whose main actors were trees that they stripped and showed their naked bodies. But today was different. Everything did not look so beautiful, and the garden opposite showed a sad picture of sadness and loneliness. The sound of the rain refreshed the movement of sorrow in my soul and heart.

Involuntarily, I touched my cheeks to make sure that what I was feeling was the tears in my eyes that colluded with the rain and fell together. There was no time to let the tears disrupt the autumn programs. So slowly, with my eyes fixed on the bed next to the wall where the most beautiful song of my life rested, I made sure that she was not aware of my broken heart. I was successful. She lay as calmly as possible on the bed like a pleasant spring, as if her feverish body was screaming the heat of summer. I quickly dried my cheeks to hide everything that was going on inside me. Then I went to her and knelt in front of her. But it was not easy to breathe with her under one roof and prevent your eyes from raining. I could not control myself. Her hands were on her chest, and she waited in complete calm, as she burned in the heat, until her physical reserve was exhausted. I could even hear the sound of her burning, which was hotter and hotter than the wood inside the fireplace. It was not difficult to measure the amount of fever. I didn't even have to put my hand on her forehead. The redness of her cheeks and her erratic breath testified that she was trying hard to calm my heart with her presence. But as if she was alone, she continued to be restless. What with the feeling of beauty, she was asleep and even in these circumstances she had not forgotten me! Snow-white dress that I first met in the snowy season of this garden, with a light make-up and the only ornament she wore, Tamimah. On the first day I met her, I saw her with a thin chain around her hand that was attached to her middle finger. I asked her to always wear it in her hand, because just as she herself seemed special to me, so did her adornment, and now, at the last moment, she had worn it to remind him of the whole time, who had spent with him.

I looked at my watch. Various medicines were next to the bed. There was little time left until the hour of using the pills that the doctor had prescribed just to ease the way, and she had nothing but sleep and rest, which was devoid of reality. I touched her face and got up involuntarily and suddenly because I could not bear to witness any more incident that was happening slowly. I went to the fireplace. I could see her beautiful face in the flames, burning brighter than them. It was the second day in a row that the situation had reached its maximum bitterness and the minutes were moving forward like clockwork, and although I was eager for their slowness so that my companion would not end, the fear of her end destroyed the calm of seconds and minutes. I was not in a good condition mentally and physically. I knew that my desire for tomorrow was dead and that I was going to have a hard time. I even thought for a moment that maybe it's me that needs pity and attention, because I was in great pain. I did not believe in any miracle and saw how my hopes gave way to despair at every moment, and this was a natural flow and no one and no force could stand against it. Yesterday, when the doctor came to her bedside for the last time, his confused face made me realise that it is better not to disturb her more than this.

I went back to the window; it was as if my only connection to life. Like prison birds, I crawled through the old walls of the villa, feeling ashamed and remorseful for not being able to do anything. I looked at the garden again. My eyes were involuntarily looking for a dream in which joy and vivacity were rippling. In disbelief, I saw a garden outside the window with large green trees, each with summer fruits and light all over. The awesomeness of the garden was a little different. The building next to the garden wall was new and the yard was covered with new paving. The pool water also shone in the sun. Moments of excitement took over my whole being. I could not have a correct understanding of time and place. I could hear my heart pounding louder than ever. I felt a cold sweat on my forehead. Suddenly, I came to believe that I was seeing my future, and maybe this is my future, and I am now walking in the past, and maybe I am remembering a memory and looking back at the memories of the past. I tried to concentrate as much as possible. There were two children running among the trees in the garden, and there was a chair on the porch of the villa, from which I could not see who she was. Then I found myself standing in front of the window again, looking out from behind at the vibrant summer view of the garden. Both children were playing and the fatherly feeling in my heart rippled when I saw them. I made sure that the future belonged to me, and in those circumstances, nothing but joy awaited me and that sorrow would surely end, and perhaps this promising dream would be that she would rise from the bed and watch the journey with me. But why did I step on the memories of the past? Maybe I wanted to remind myself of a time when I never wanted it to happen again, and its memories have been revisited just to appreciate my current life with my wife. I came to the bed happy and confident of what had come before my eyes to promise her the bright days. I wanted to say that we have won and that the period of pain and illness has passed and that I have seen her in my future dream, that we are having a happy time with each other and our children in the reconstructed villa, and that sadness is no longer there. I came to the bed. I stood motionless for a moment. I did not know what to say. My eyes could not comprehend what I saw. I did not know if I had dreamed wrongly or had emotional errors. Her clasped hands were no longer together, and her cheeks turned yellow. Her head was tilted slightly and the fever had disappeared from her body. I was not sure how long I had been standing by the window, but I knew it was not long because it was not yet time for the next medication. Slowly and hesitantly, I sat down on the bed next to her and looked at her hands without disturbing her. There was no movement and she was lying lifeless on her last station. With trembling hands, I took her hand and gently pulled Tamimah out of her hand and very slowly brought it to my eyes and began to break without making a sound. I did not know why what I had seen in my dream contradicted the present incident. I felt suffocated. I could not breathe well. It was as if the air she was breathing provided me with the oxygen I needed. The present dream had become a nightmare that had taken over my whole being. Yes, she left me forever. I got up and went to the building. I wanted to get some fresh air. I could not breathe anymore. I ran to the door. Fear had taken over my whole being. I opened the door. A fresh breeze hit my face and caressed my sweaty face. Suddenly, I saw in front of me two children playing and my wife sitting on a chair and now looking at me in surprise. She got up and came towards me. She looked at me. Then she took my hand, which was tied, and opened it gently. She looked at me again and calmly rubbed my face and said, "Why are you sweating so much? What did you hold in your hand? Beauty chains. For whom?"

And I closed the door behind me to say goodbye to my memories, involuntarily handed it to her, and with a smile, while looking at my children, I said, "Tamimah."

Ash Wednesday

Ash Wednesday[*]

He left the room and went to a dish in which there was the ashes of the burnt Sunday Crosses of the palm trees. He picked it up and went back to the room and the person in it, pointing to him and pointing out that it was better to get out. So he took his hand for help and led him out of the room. Then he stood in front of him and put his finger into the dish and put it on his forehead and drew the cross carefully. Then he smiled at him and shook his hand, as if to reassure him that everything would be fine these days and that God would surely hear his heartfelt voice. The man, with tears in his eyes and swallowing his hatred, nodded and tried to thank

---

[*]**Ash Wednesday** or Wednesday of Repentance: The first day of Lent (forty days of Catholic Christian fasting) is in the Western Christian calendar, which occurs forty-six days before Easter. Since it depends on Easter, it happens on a different date every year and people fast on that day. The name of this day is derived from placing ashes on the foreheads of believers as a sign of mourning and repentance before God. The ashes are usually collected from the Palm Sunday burns of the previous year. This day is the day after Tuesday, the confession.

the priest. The priest then led him to the exit and waited to invite someone else to the confessional. This time, a tall man with long hair and a black suit appeared in front of him. He did not look very old, he looked middle-aged, but he looked healthier than his age.

"I have had many illusions for some time. Of course, it cannot be said that it is an illusion. In fact, an inner force has brought me here today. I do not feel calm, and during this time, I feel that many times I have strayed from the moral framework. Of course, I have never been a religious person, but frequent slips caused me to lose my self-confidence and constantly feel the shadow of depression and anxiety on myself. A few years ago, while I was working in an office company, one of my clients offered me a financial case. Well, at that time, I was not in a good condition, and of course, I was younger and the dream of wealth had taken over my whole being. The truth is, I did not even think about the consequences and accepted it very quickly. It is true that everything went well and no danger happened, and I gained a lot of wealth this way, but I mostly blame myself for not thinking about their offer for even a few minutes and accepting it very quickly. It was not too hard work. They just wanted me to ignore them a little bit during their case, and of course, I was sure that no one would be harmed. The only thing that worried me was that no one would be harmed in this way. After finishing this project,

I decided to leave that company and start a personal business with the money I earned. I spent some time in that company so that my sudden absence and leaving there would not seem to others. A few months later, when I was sure that everything was in order, I resigned and received a salary for the few years I had worked there honestly. I was very happy and laughed in my heart when I got the redemption amount. Then I quickly got back to what I had been thinking about for a few months and quickly expanded my business. Everything went very well until some time ago, while passing in front of the medicine company where I was working, I saw that the factory was closed. Although I had promised myself that I would never go back, the curiosity and what happened to me from there that became my launching pad made me ask a little question about it. I soon realised that a few years ago, a group had introduced a large amount of counterfeit drugs into the factory's economic and production cycle, which after a while, due to the consequences it had on patients, caused many catastrophes. Of course, I'm sure I did not interfere, and what I was doing as a quality controller was done so precisely that it happened only once, and when I compare the timing with the closing time of the factory, I find no connection. In fact, I have nothing to do with the factory, but I do not know why after that day, the feeling of joy and happiness left me. I am very successful in my business and of course very generous. Many employees are now making a living through the business I have built and are very happy to have a successful manager like me running them. To be honest, I have added a significant amount to their salaries since that day, but I still feel guilty. Father, I ask you to help me and ask for forgiveness. I know that I am completely innocent in this matter, but a kind of feeling of dissatisfaction has taken over my whole being and has darkened my heart. To show my generosity to the church, I bring an envelope with which I donate it. Inside the envelope is a bank cheque that can be used to handle some church affairs. Maybe this will improve my mental state. However, I still feel that I am just delusional."

He came out of the room and went to the ashtray and picked it up and returned to the man. His face was more tired than when he entered the confessional. It was as if he had devoted all his energy to convincing the Holy Father that he was innocent, or that he saw the priest as the voice of his conscience that he should attract his attention. Although the priest did not pay attention to what he said, the man felt satisfied, and after the cross was engraved on his forehead, he hugged the Holy Father and squeezed him a little. Then he took the envelope out of his coat pocket and happily handed it to the priest. The priest also involuntarily accompanied the man with his eyes until he left.

"In fact, my mood is not good at all. This should not have happened. Our relationship is so much better than trying to figure it out. We understand each other well. But the situation is different. I do not know what to say. All I know is that I have to tell you this so that my sins may be forgiven. Of course, it cannot be called a sin, but why it is a sin, it is better not to deceive myself anymore. We would love to start life together formally, but you know the economic situation is not at all normal. During these one or two years, we tried very hard to control everything and start a home and life with the savings we make. But sometimes things do not go well. I am very careful, but I do not know why this happened. Certainly, God forgives us because we did not want to bring someone else into this life like ourselves. No need to think. As time went on, I felt that the guilt of this work was increasing and he was moving towards more evolution. I had to stop it. At any price I could. The same day I found out, we went to one or two doctors together, and after getting the necessary advice, without having to think about keeping him, without a doubt, we both decided to take action the next day and have a child abortion what was unintentionally created. Holy Father, God forgives us. Make sure it is. He was only two months old and had not yet formed. God knows how hard it is for people like us to live and how difficult it is for us to make a living. I know he forgives us, and all my joy was on Ash Wednesday to come here and confess and repent of the sin I have unintentionally committed so that I do not do it again. I hope I find peace when you draw the cross of ashes on my forehead. I urge you to pray for the peace of both of us."

He slowly drew the ash cross on her forehead and without feeling on his face indicated that she would be forgiven. Then he put the ashtray in its place and entered the confession room.

"I do not feel good when I look in the mirror. I am one of the influential people in this city, and in order not to be recognised, I put on a hat and covered my face. I did not want anyone to know who I am. Even you, the Holy Father, are going to ask forgiveness for me. While I was in office, I thought I had enough time for a lot of work. But soon everything changed. Well, like many others, I started with myself. You know, I'm not upset about that at all because I was working hard. I tried to calm everyone down day and night. It was my right to enjoy relative peace and well-being. This is something that is common everywhere, I am one like the others. Gradually, I became more powerful and had more possibilities. I decided to set aside some savings for myself so that when I moved, I would not think about my future and know that I could spend the rest of my life easily. This made some of my opponents aware. I am not a violent person at all and reject violence at all. But they made me do something I never liked. Holy Father, believe me, I did not want to harm them. They should not have explored. I think you understand who I'm talking about. I instructed one of my deputies to scare them a little so that they would be careful about their behaviour. But it seems that this issue is facing their resistance and a fight was taking place, and my deputy is forced to kill both of them so that no trace remains. Holy Father, this city is not big enough for you to be unaware of. I mean the same two people whose bodies were found down the river three weeks ago, and next to them was the body of my deputy with a gun that was later found. I did not want to kill him, but I was sure that if they came looking for the killer of the two, the deputy would definitely introduce me to them and say that he had taken orders from me. In fact, it was the deputy's right to be killed because I told him to scare them only a little, not to kill them. He had exaggerated. Basically, when I think about it more closely, I come to the conclusion that maybe there was a personal settlement between them and maybe the issue had nothing to do with me at all. I think about it a lot, but I cannot get rid of it. Holy Father, I desperately ask you to ask forgiveness for me. I have never been infected with such a sin. However, I still doubt that I may not have chosen the right person for this mission. Holy Father, I know they both had families. I have brought you a sum of money as compensation to give to them as you see fit, without specifying where it came from. Of course, I know you did not notice me and did not know me. In order not to reveal my identity, I put the money in a suitcase in cash and placed it next to the confession room. You are the trustee of these people. Act as you see fit. Also, do not leave the confession room because I do not want to be seen. I will just bring you a dish of ashes, and as you sit there, cross the ashes on my forehead so that my repentance may be accepted and I may be forgiven."

The priest left the confession room and went to the church. No one was in church anymore. For almost a long time, he listened to the confessions of others on Ash Wednesday. He looked tired. He went inside and changed his clothes to escape his holy form. He went to the suitcase and opened it. The inside of the suitcase was full of unfolded bundles of banknotes. He touched them a little. His grey fingers blackened them a little. Then he looked at his fingers. Then he took out the envelope he had in his pocket and pulled the cheque out of it. He took it in his hand. He touched the amount of the cheque with the same hand that drew the ash cross on the foreheads of the confessors. It seemed remarkable. He put it back in his pocket. Then he took the suitcase in his hand, and with the other hand, he carried the suitcase of his clothes that he had collected and moved towards the exit. He stood and looked around the confessional. He thought to himself that he might have a year to confess and repent to Holy Father in the next Ash Wednesday of a city no one knows.

Cross(Chalipa)

Cross (Chalipa[*])

"Hereby informs our dear compatriots that the Resistance Front has achieved many victories yesterday, and we hope that this process will continue so that we can fight the Invading Forces and even liberate the occupied parts. Therefore, the received news indicates that the course of the war has changed and the Resistance Front will continue its fight more determined than ever, and we are sure that we will bring good news soon, and this is exactly what all the people of the country are waiting for

---

Cross (Chalipa): The Chalipa, which means the cross, is a symbol and statue of Christianity. This symbol in Aryan culture means good luck and rebirth. Some have called it one of the signs of the God Tammuz. The God Tammuz is actually another name for the sun (Tammuz sun). Dehkhoda's dictionary states: "The cross is a wood that the Christians tie in a belt and in Persian it is called a Chalipa (crucifix) and it is written that the Chalipa is the cross." The Persian Chalipa or cross is called the great wall of Naghsh-e Rostam, in which four crosses more than sixty metres high are carved on the wall of the mountain.

listening to it and participate in all fields for complete victory. Accept this congratulation from us."

*****

He turned the radio off. Suddenly, silence filled the room. Moments passed like this, but he could hear every word of the radio speaker again in the same absolute silence. A great event had taken place that was unimaginable. Many months had passed and a lot of blood was flowing, so that these few simple sentences could be heard on the radio. Perhaps for those who were not harmed in the war or were not geographically affected, it was merely information coming from a war zone. But for him, who had spent all day and night struggling all this time and witnessed the most violent scenes in human history, this news was more than just information that the speaker eagerly uttered on the radio. Maybe all the people should have put themselves in his shoes for a few minutes to realise the greatness of the work and know that this news was the ultimate dream of his that was coming true. Perhaps that day was one of the few times he sat in a rocking chair with a hot coffee in his hand and listened to the war news. All this time, he had spent his days and nights in the heat and cold of war, and now that he was on leave for a few days to regain his weakened strength, he could have held a small feast and sweetened this blessed event for himself. Lately, he has been guessing that the Resistance Force is working with double motivation and will definitely be able to have a celebration with his other comrades soon. It seemed that the Invading Forces, due to the prolongation of the war on the one hand and the hard fighting of the Resistance Forces on the other hand, had entered a state of erosion and their forces were weakening every day and there was no way for them to return. It is as if they have sunk into a swamp, and with each passing moment, they sink deeper with each struggle. They had even destroyed the bridges behind them and closed the doors of negotiations to themselves and the Resistance Forces in the very first days of their aggression. It seemed almost impossible that there was still time to negotiate. They, too, were certainly thinking of the failure that was within their reach. If this were not the case, some of their forces would not have been called back, and that was all he had experienced as a military man. He knew what the outcome would be for him and the war. He picked up the cup of coffee from the table and held it to his nose to inhale the steam and make sure it was fresh and hot. Then he tasted a sip of it, and after tasting it, he put it back on the table and at the same time put pressure on the ground with one of his legs to move the rocking chair. He was thinking that he was a soldier and that his vacation and rest time were over, and of course, even if his vacation did not end, it was his turn to go back to his comrades and fight side by side. That is, where he belongs. Eagerly like someone who listens to music and reads it to himself, he repeated the words 'be happy' to himself several times, and while tapping a certain rhythm with his fingers on the handle of the chair, interestingly, a kind of joy took of his whole being. The scars of the war were still visible on parts of his left hand, and he looked at it for a moment as a sign that he was remembering something, and he subconsciously turned his left hand and overthrew it with a determined look to make sure that he is self-satisfied and all his efforts during this period have not been in vain and victory is just a few steps away. He also thought for a moment that nothing could be more important and valuable to a fighter than the outcome of the war, and he experienced these moments in the most difficult conditions of his life. Difficult days, each of which was full of numerous and unfortunate events and incidents, each of which was enough to disappoint any fighter. But with what strong will, he had set foot on the field that he had never hesitated to continue on his way, with all his mental and physical fatigue. However, sometimes he heard about the failure of his comrades and even saw a few people who left this great battle and hid in the noise of war and saved their lives. But these, too, did not diminish the courage of others and showed their competence to achieve the same important goal. Even he himself was a living witness to this, and this eyewitness could honestly and decisively reveal the mysterious path that the Resistance Force never thinks of defeat and knows how to defend his land and save it. In any case, the blood of all those young people should not be trampled. The blood of those who were innocent every day, just because they wanted to defend their homeland, was shed, and their half-souled souls calmed down one by one with a rhythmic rhythm on the defenceless and neutral ground. Soon, however, the storm of war, along with a torrential downpour of explosives, ended their calm, tearing their lifeless bodies to pieces and leaving nothing to remember their parents. This story was repeated day and night, and every night, he wondered if he too would be eaten by the earth, or if he would survive to embrace victory and celebrate it, knowing that this several months' resistance had been sacred and in no way his time has not been wasted. Because in every war, he would hear whispers from those around him saying that it is better for him to be neutral and avoid this controversy. The great powers are at loggerheads, and his presence as a trivial tool will bring nothing but future frustrations. But he was a man of war. A military feels empty without a real war and always waits to test its strength and show that it was created for the hard days, not what people experience in their lifetime. Hard days with the blood of thousands of people and many tears waiting to land. Whether these tears are from the companions of the Resistance Front or from the loved ones who are waiting for the victory of their youth against the Invading Force. Both will suffer the innocent bloodshed that is expected of any war. When a fire of war breaks out, many innocent people burn in it like good firewood, conveying their warmth to other people's bodies and makes them feverish. He recalls that a few days ago, on his way back for a short three-day break, he saw a teenager lying motionless on the ground with nothing but parts of his lifeless body, and his youth, despite being a few days under the sun, was recognisable, and the ideal he pursued was admirable to him. He was happy that even seeing such scenes did not stop him from pursuing his ideals and, on the contrary, made him more determined to achieve the final victory, even if a lifeless teenager falls to the ground or an accident happens to him. He had prepared himself for the most difficult days and always said to himself that a fighter must accept the possible dangers and hardships with open arms and should not doubt or abandon his goal and ideal. He revisited the idealistic slogans he heard every day on his pocket radio about struggle and success and saw it as part of a sacred struggle in which he had to sacrifice even his own life and what could be more than that for the ideals of the Resistance Front. Now, with this victory and the promises of future victory, the necessity of advancing to the soil of the aggressors was gradually felt so that they would see the result of their work in action and they would kneel and see the soil of their land in the arms of the Resistance Force. He no longer had to wait. The waiting time was over and he had to get up and join them. His friends were waiting for him, and he thought that he should step on the battlefield as strong as he could and fight with all his might against the violence of the Invading Forces and shed their blood so that perhaps peace would return to him and his thoughts. Thoughts that were confusing and sometimes made him doubt. He looked across the room from the rocking chair. His military uniforms hung behind the door, waiting for him. His eyes lit up, and at the same time, he put his hand to his chest and squeezed the cross around his neck, as if to evoke a covenant, he pressed the cross firmly in his fist for a moment and then read the sentences under his lips, as if he was praying, and this was exactly the concoction that prepared him for the busy future days, and he would take on any change in his perspective. It is as if he is satisfied with that thinking and no longer needs to be in the place of others and make sure that the work he is doing is evaluated positively or negatively. However, if he again put himself in the place of the aggressor soldiers because of his logic, he would feel that they too were right, and that would be the end of his beliefs. Perhaps if he were not a military man, his thoughts would not have seemed so harsh. In fact, he felt that he had never been in the military and that these were all waves that had always flowed in his mind and nurtured a sense of revenge. A kind of energy that persuaded him to wear a military uniform instead of an ordinary citizen and to attack the aggressors side by side with the Resistance Forces and with great intensity and to take revenge on each and every one of them and take the blood of innocent loved ones and their families from sinners and those who committed it. It no longer mattered to him who or what had lined up in front of him. They will be sentenced to death, regardless of age or circumstance, and he will execute it and give any thought to his mind to achieve it.

*****

Now that the voice of the radio announcer had calmed him down a little and healed his sense of revenge, he remembered the old days when he lived quietly in this small room with his loved ones and could not figure out exactly what had really happened. A bloody battle ensued, and he and his family were so geographically unlucky that he was at the centre of gravity between the two countries, swallowing up his home and making them war victims waiting to die. This misfortune was so obvious that when he saw the vacancies of his loved ones around him, he wondered if he had committed a sin that was cursed by the politicians of his time and simply walked as far as possible on the path of geographical force and this exorbitant cost has paid? Numerous bombs were threatening his family home every day, heavier than the day before, and he wondered if their voices were loud enough for the Red Cross to hear and reach for the wounded. The wounds of war seemed so great that even the Red Cross could not heal it if it had come to the rescue. He reached again for a cross with a string of black leather around his neck, and with sorrowful eyes, he hoped that the Red Cross could step in and save them from the atmosphere of today's societies, each with its own colourful slogans to say we are right. Slogans that were spread with great excitement among the people to conceal the culmination of the war, and how painful it is that in these few months he has been in this dark room, devoid of any facilities, waiting at any moment for one of those bombs, as if he chooses his victims, go to him and swallow the rest of his life. He recalled last month when he experienced the biggest attack in his life, when the invading gangs came in after bombing the city and rejoiced in the back alleys of the city, rejoicing in their success. However, it did not last long and the Resistance Forces reached the city. In the days leading up to the fall, he hid in the attic, watching outside from a small window as blood flowed through the city and the unusual laughter of men echoed through the narrow streets of the city, and in this critical case, how many days he could actually be hidden in the corner. But the pain of losing his family could not put him in this situation forever. The sound of roaring inside the city was spread, and fortunately, the city returned to its former state, although it was nothing like before. The damage caused by the advance of the Invading Forces was so great that it turned the city into a ruin. Sleeping in a place where it could be pregnant at any time by an unpleasant accident kept him awake until morning, and he fell asleep when he could no longer fear and fainted in his place, and when he opened his eyes, he smelled death and ruins with all his being. He felt the grief of losing his loved ones that came back to him.

*****

He got up. He had been sitting in a rocking chair for a long time and needed to stand up and feel safe. During this time, he had pushed the chair back and forth so fast that instability had taken over his whole being. So he stopped suddenly and then began to walk the length and width of the room. He came to the window and stared unnoticed at the deserted streets of the city as if plagued. There was no more news about the people of the city. A group had gone to the brink of death and destruction, and some had left the city in fear. A group hid in the buildings, and some volunteered to join the Resistance Forces, taking up arms while not receiving military training and going to war with the same sense of revenge. But violence and revenge and killing others was not something he could handle. So more desperately than ever, he thought that if he lived far away, he might be relatively safe and not feel so much fear and the smell of destruction. That was exactly his motivation, now that he was sheltering in a room a few hundred kilometres from the critical point of the war, listening to a radio announcer. He was a citizen who was fortunately far from the battlefield, and other compatriots were involved.

He turned the radio off. The speaker's cheerful voice gave him hope and motivation again. He now spends several months in this room, away from the repetitive sounds of tanks and bombs. But he could not close his eyes to the people who are at the critical point of the war and under the constant pressure of annihilation. He saw his heart filled with compassionate feelings that rolled against his fellow human beings at that boundary between blood and fire. He could not stand indifferently and watch, but he knew that nothing was made of him and that he could do nothing but stay and look and that all he could do for them was to kneel and carry the cross around his neck. He grabs it by the hand and implores to ask his Creator to put an end to this bloodshed, designed by the ambitious. He repeated the same thing for hours during the day to get results, and of course, he did not neglect his life. Now that he was in a few hundred kilometres of chaos, he should not imprison himself. The affairs of his life call him to himself. But he never stopped praying for them and did not take his cross off his chest. The thought that he too could be in the same space, or that the war would take place where he was also present, would surely change his circumstances, and how fortunate he was that he was geographically friendly with him, and at least, he was a few hundred miles from the fire and blood. Although there was no guarantee that he would survive there, the efforts of the Resistance Front, along with the news that the speaker was broadcasting from moment to moment, gave him the guarantee that he was safe from the current dangers and that he should pray for the end. Out of sympathy, he reduced some of his food and used it to help the injured. The famine had aggravated the situation so much that he realised that even in the cities far from the centre of the war, the situation was still dire. The whole city was in ruins and death, and all that was seen was the inability of the people who had made heroes in their minds and followed them. Unaware that in fact they themselves are heroes who rush to join Resistance Force and participate with others without military uniforms. But he could not do so because he had a problem with the concept of war, and he could do nothing but pity the injured. In any case, he and his position were not so unstable that he wanted to forget everything and enter the field ruthlessly. Perhaps he did not see this passion for presence and participation as appropriate to his situation, which in fact excluded him from this caravan and gave him the justification that sometimes help and participation does not mean physical presence but can be achieved through prayer and contentment and send his surplus consumption obtained from his savings. This is perhaps the best way to support those who are currently in geographical force and being invaded by Invading Forces. Forces that presented their performance in such a way that they also considered themselves to achieve the ideals of their country and considered their work sacred and did not spare any effort to achieve it. Certainly people who are in the military, or in that geographical force, or like him, a few hundred kilometres from the point of crisis, also face the same problem on the other side of the war.

*****

While he knew that the coffee on the table was completely cold, he took it and drank it to refresh his breath and get out of his mind. It had been a long time since the newscaster had said happily, and he was now thinking that he was doing the best he could do, and now that he did not believe in politicians who could not put problems aside through interaction and dialogue, they turn to bloody human

58

wars, and now that he is not capable enough to correct their thinking, it is better, as the smallest part of a society, to distance himself from the polluted environments that are on fire and destruction at the hands of their politicians. Yes, he was a refugee. It was time to think that he could not change the rotten thoughts of those whose minds were filled with violence. He cannot make even a small move to establish stability and peace. He does not even believe in war and is completely unfamiliar with military science. On the other hand, he loves to live and enjoy this divine gift. What difference does it make that some people call him a coward and slander him? It is important for him to stand in front of a window now and in the same room as before but with the difference that this time the window is open and peace and quiet are passing through it. And this is while he has a cross around his neck and in front of it is a flag that plays the role of the same cross and dances in the wind in the air and shows the beautiful taste of peace and tranquillity, without having to feel sorry for anyone or endanger himself or lose loved ones. Even if he is called a coward.

Four Leaf Clover

Four Leaf Clover*

She hurried to the gate of the residence. She waved to the guard and entered the yard. She could feel the cold autumn air well. Breathing, she passed through a corridor surrounded on both sides by tall, dead trees. She could hear the sound of the leaves of the trees beneath her feet and the steam of the breaths that walked ahead of her. The leaves were painted with a colourful carpet of different colours. The sound of the wind blows through the trees and moves the leaves in front of her. The sky was grey and the clouds in the sky promised a cold autumn day. It seemed that it was winter in this part of the city and maybe her clothes were not

---

*__Four Leaf Clover:__ *The result of abnormal changes in three leaf clover. The three-leaf clover was used as a symbol for the Christian trinity by St Patrick. According to tradition, finding four leaf clover is a sign of good luck. Especially, if it is found by chance by the person. Some believe that the leaf is a symbol of something: the first leaf: Faith; second leaf: Hope; third leaf: Love and the fourth leaf: Chance.*

suitable for this weather. But it did not take long for her to remember that the clothes she wore were the only choices she had and wore. Maybe it would have been better for her to think a little about herself and put aside contentment and prepare a suitable dress for winter with the salary of this month. Anyway, there was nothing left until the end of the month. With a smile of satisfaction at what she had promised, she climbed the stairs of the building and reached the main door. She hoped that the Lady and the Gentleman of the House would not notice her delay or at least that other servants had filled her vacancy. It was rare for her to make a mistake in scheduling her work, but it had been a while since, at the suggestion of one of her co-workers, she had taken a number of chores to do at home every night after returning home and considered as a financial aid. Although the Lady and the Gentleman of the House were good people and supported her a lot, but her current situation was not such that it could be compensated and changed with this support. That's why she spent a lot of time doing them last night and stayed up late. On the other hand, her work during the day was intense and tedious and did not leave much time for her, and she had a special sensitivity and had to be very careful to maintain it. She worked for both the Lady and the Gentleman of the House for a long time, and after the birth of their first child, she was considered a babysitter. The care of the child required great time, and her work became more difficult when she was entrusted with the care of the second child the following year. This was done six days a week and lasted from eight in the morning until eight in the afternoon. She took care of the children and sometimes helped the lady with some of her personal matters because of the lady's interest in her. Of course, it was a sign of their attention and trust that the babysitter was involved in the internal affairs of the home. Therefore, given such a position, she should be more cautious and adjust to her current situation. From the point of view of the Lady and the Gentleman of the House, everything can be compensated and forgiven except disorder and carelessness. So the babysitter was responsible for the delay that happened that morning and wanted to have a good excuse for the delay today, if need be.

The gardener was washing the porch of the residence and after noticing her presence, he raised his head and greeted her with a smile. She knew this kind of respect from others because of her special place in front of the Lady and the Gentleman of the House, and she thought that nothing more should be expected because of the importance of her job. So she waved her hand and entered the building. There was a certain excitement inside the residence, and all the servants were busy preparing the reception hall. Surprisingly, she noticed the presence of the Lady of the House at that time with the servants in the morning. The residence was run by three maids, a cook, a guard and a gardener with her as a babysitter. The cook and her daughter, who was considered a servant, lived with the guard at the residence, and the rest, like her, left after eight o'clock at night. Usually, the Lady of the House would go to her room after breakfast and paint or do her personal chores, but that morning's rush to arrange the maids in front of the Lady of the House was a little frightening. She immediately went to her and lowered her head in respect and greeted her, waiting for any warning from her. The Lady of the House turned to her and looked at her, raised her face with her hand and smiled, and at the same time shook her head to show her that there was nothing to worry about. Although this behaviour on the part of the Lady of the House was normal, she was aware of her sensitivities and knew that ignoring her children out of disorder was not something that could be easily overlooked. Then the Lady of the House went on to say that she did not need to bother herself too much today and that a party would be held in the residence hall today, and she should be present at the party as well. Until now, she has not attended the Lady and the Gentleman of the House's night parties and always left after work. She was completely confused and the events were incomprehensible to her. In order to hide her surprise from the eyes of the Lady of the House, she immediately said, "Definitely, madam. Whatever you say." But suddenly, she remembered her clothes that were not suitable for the party, and she did not even know who the guests were and why she was there.

The Lady of the House, who had predicted everything, pointed to the package on the table and said, "These clothes are for you. You can wear them to a party. Also, do not worry about children. Of course, they are at the party. In other words, the reason for the party is basically what they want. That's why I felt that your presence could make them happy too. So today, after having lunch with the kids, you can go to the maid's room and relax a bit and get ready for the party. The children will be with me from three o'clock onwards. I would like to take care of their work today."

The babysitter, as if answering all her questions, took a deep breath and made sure that something or someone did not threaten her work, and that even the Lady of the House was so busy at the night party that she did not notice her delay. Maintaining this job was very important to her and all the affairs of her life were from the income she earns from this work. She should have been more careful. In the current situation, it was much more difficult to find a new job. Thinking that everything was in order, happiness took over her whole being. Then the Lady of the House shook her hand a little and said to her in a loving manner: "I would like you to be very beautiful tonight, because some friends are also invited to this party. This is also the request of the children. It could be a great experience for them to host a party as they wish."

The Babysitter replied happily, "Surely, it will be so, madam." Then she went to the package and picked it up very soon and took it with her to the maids' rest room and put it in a corner. She spent the whole afternoon dreaming of what to expect in the package, and as the Lady of the House had requested, she delivered the children to their mother at three o'clock and immediately descended the stairs and went to the restroom. There was plenty of time left until the party and she could calmly open the package and examine the clothes inside. She even thought about sleeping a little to look good at night so that she would have good energy during the party. This was the first party she attended after all these years. Although she was a babysitter, she felt that a long time had passed since she last attended a party and that the party could distract her a little from her daily routine.

She opened the package in a hurry. She did not expect to see things in a large package that she could not even imagine.

Beautiful and long blue dress with white flowers, suitable shoes with clothes and a beautiful shawl made of leather. She was so excited. Next to it was a small box. She looked at it first. Then she picked it up. It was as if she did not want this excitement to end. She checked the box several times. Then she opened the box very carefully so that it would not be damaged. There was a brooch inside. She took it out. The brooch was silver in colour and had a strange design. The design of a four leaf clover was on it, which shone with white jewels on it. She told herself that this brooch definitely has a special glow at night and under the light of chandeliers. Even its special design was interesting to her. She could not believe that such a day was waiting for her. She considered the four leaf clover as a sign of good luck. This became more prominent for her when she put on her clothes and stared at the flowers on them. The white flowers on the dress were also four leaf clover, which created a special harmony next to the brooch. She looked in the small mirror in the room and tried to look at all the clothes. She had never had such a garment in her entire life, and she could guess its approximate price from its brand. Undoubtedly, after the party, the clothes were for her and she could take them with her. But whatever she thought, she did not know where to use it again. She was too busy to attend a party or those around her did not have the opportunity to invite her at all. But having it also motivated her to be happy, and she knew that even if she hung it in her house and in her closet, she would still feel good.

Then she took the bag out of the package and threw it on her hand. In front of the mirror, she went back and forth several times and tried to measure all aspects of the dress. She liked the Lady of the House very much and was happy that she had measured the dress so accurately for her, and she said to herself, "These are all signs of the Lady of the House's care and attention and that she wished that this morning's delay would never happen again." Although wearing the dress for a few hours at the party bothered her, she never liked to take it off and wear it again at the party. She even forgot that she had thought about sleeping for an hour before opening the package. She did not like to replace the existing excitement with something. On the other hand, the children remembered that they had caused so much excitement and thought that it would be better to pay more attention to them from now on. The party started at seven o'clock, and the babysitter entered the hall in a beautiful dress. Along the way, beautiful flowers appeared in the pots and the smell of food could be smelled from everywhere. The fruit bowls were beautifully decorated and attracted everyone's attention along with the sweets. The table in front of her was full of colourful snacks that tempted the guests. She had a strange feeling, especially when she saw other servants looking at her with regret and she walking among them so proudly. There was a strange contradiction. On the one hand, she liked to be like the Lady and the Gentleman of the House and other guests and not pay attention to them, but on the other hand, she was like them until a few hours ago and she became like them again after the party. She tried not to pay attention to this issue, and at least at this party and in these few hours, she treated as she always liked. She even thought for a moment that she deserved all these conditions, and that made her happy and hoped that this process would continue. It seemed that it was better to strengthen her faith and continue her life with double hope and love. She even had plans in mind that she had to implement as soon as possible.

The Lady and the Gentleman of the House were sitting at the top of the hall with the children, and as soon as they saw her, the children ran towards her, and she hugged them with special interest. Then they went with them to the other guests. When she reached the Lady and the Gentleman of the House, she was polite and sat among them in the form of a maiden with special confidence and at the lady's request. She was very careful not to wrinkle her beautiful clothes when sitting down and to position herself so that everyone could see her brooch, which was very special. The Lady of the House welcomed her and introduced her to the others. They greeted her one after another. She felt great to be the centre of attention of others. For the first time, she felt that she could stand among others and even speak and that others would listen to her and confirm her by shaking their heads. Of course, the way the Lady of the House was introduced was not ineffective. The Lady of the House, when introducing her, had made her a heroine who is in control of all circumstances and does not know what to do without her. She even mentioned her as a member of their family in one of her speeches and spoke about the children's dependence and eloquence. Although she sometimes envied the Lady of the House, she now loved her with all her being. After a while, the Lady of the House pointed to one of the maids. She immediately left the hall and after a short time entered the hall with a beautiful cake. At that moment, all the guests stood up and the babysitter did the same. Everyone started clapping while looking at her. The Lady of the House hugged her with a special sincerity and the children jumped up and down happily around them. Then everyone sang 'Happy Birthday' together. During these years, she was so lonely that she did not remember when her birthday was. In fact, she had no experience of having a birthday party and did not know what to do. There were tears in her eyes. She could not believe that she had been treated like this. Of course, she was very pleased that the Lady and the Gentleman of the House paid so much attention to her, but she did not think that it was so important for them to have such a party for her. The children circled around her with great excitement. "We told Mom to have a party for your birthday." One of them approached the babysitter and hugged her softly. The Lady of the House also looked at her children happily. The Gentleman of the House was also having fun and talking and laughing with the other guests. Time passed quickly and she liked time to stand still. She did not want that night to end at all. All this time, the babysitter was looking at the four leaf clover on her dress and the brooch, and on the other hand, she was looking at the children and their happiness. One of the maids was also providing services for her. There was a strange contradiction in her. At this time, the Lady of the House stood among the others and announced that the babysitter had paid a lot of attention to their family over the past few years and that the party was held after her presence and the joy of the children. Then everyone clapped and congratulated her.

It was time for dinner and the party was coming to an end. The Lady of the House pointed to a maid to guide the children to their room to rest. Little by little, the guests left the hall one after the other, and the babysitter, thinking that these events had taken place in reality and was coming to an end, went to the Lady and the Gentleman of the House and thanked them for that night. No one was in the hall anymore, and the babysitter had to get ready to get on the last bus. Because if she lost it, she would have to pay a lot for the taxi. Her place of residence was the last bus stop that took her there every day, and the last departure was at 11.30. She should never lose it. Going by taxi made her pay all the money she had left until the end of the month, and the situation was worse than it was. She hurried to the maids' resting room and immediately took off her clothes, carefully arranging them as she had taken them out of the box, as if she had never used them. During the party, she was sometimes careful not to damage it. She also removed the four leaf clover from her chest and looked at it, and as if talking to it, asked it to repeat this event one more time and return her to the way she deserves. She put it in her own box. She put on her clothes. She felt a little comfortable. She closed the box and held it tightly, then said goodbye to the other maids as if she had returned to her previous state and made her way to the exit door. At the same time, she heard a maid run to her and give her a package, saying, "This is a little food tonight. You can take it with you, and you will not need to make food tomorrow night. The Lady of the House also said that the children should go to class tomorrow at eight o'clock in the morning. Do not be late and do not repeat the issue of delay today." The maid said this and left her alone.

As if the babysitter did not believe the day was over, she stepped out of the building towards the garden and yard, holding her balance to hold her belongings along with a box of clothes and a pack of food. The autumn wind was blowing harder than in the morning and shook the big cedar trees in the yard, making a terrifying noise. The darkness of the air and the rustling of the autumn leaves made her feel the cold in her body. She added her speed as she walked quickly. She has to walk for a while to get to the bus station. With tears in her eyes, she thought she had had a very exciting day, and the reason for the tears was the winds blowing in her face. She pressed the box of clothes tighter to her chest to prevent herself from the cold wind and keep warm a little. She was happy that she had a four-leaf clover in her bag, thinking that she might be able to save her salary for a few months to buy warm clothes for the winter.

Stone Mansion

Stone Mansion

As he climbed the mountain, he glanced at the stone mansion. It had been a while since it had caught his attention. It seemed unnatural that a large and strong mansion had been built in the space between the mountains. He found no justification for it. On the other hand, he had heard many rumours in this regard. Some people believed that this mansion belonged to extra-terrestrials and no human foot had ever stepped on it. Some also believed that the mansion was abandoned and that no one had gone there for years. There were different opinions about its history. He had heard from the past that it was built by the Satan and it is better that he never even looks at it and does not set foot there. Perhaps the advice he had heard about it most motivated him to step on a mountain slope and climb it. There was not even a way to get to the mansion, and this showed that no one was present in the stone mansion. But why should a big building be built in the heart of the mountain and why no one has ever thought about what is going on inside the stone mansion. Whenever he asked the people of the city about this, he saw fear in their eyes. It was as if no one wanted to talk about it. In other words, they had digested the existence of that mansion with all its many questions and preferred to pay attention to their daily lives rather than take risks and explore the issues that the ancients had warned about. More interestingly, the influential people of the city also forbade the public to go there, believing that approaching the Satan's mansion could pose great dangers both to themselves and to others. So not only did influential people not help him in this matter but they themselves were an obstacle in his way. He recalled that once in the main square of the city, he reached out to an official who had come to visit the city and asked him about the stone mansion. He also stated without hesitation that the law has made its opinion clear in this regard and that is that no one has the right to approach the mansion, and in such an event, the law will deal severely, because in addition to endangering life himself causes many problems for residents, because this mansion is cursed.

He took a deep breath and tried not to think of the people's fears, because doubt pervaded his whole being. At first, he seemed quite determined, but the closer he got to the mansion, the more anxious he became and the more he prevented him from continuing. In order to regain his previous motivation, he thought that he was the first person to set foot in the stone mansion and that he might be able to unveil the secrets of this mansion and return to the inhabitants of the city with a full hand and be their saviour and can eliminate their horror and ignorance that have gripped them for many years. He stopped for a moment and looked at the mansion. There was still a long way to go. The path was also rugged and climbing through the rocks added to the difficulty. The direct sun was shining on him, and the heat of a summer day in the middle of a rocky mountain path had doubled the difficulty of the journey. How was it possible for them to build such a large mansion in past centuries with empty hands, without any means that can help them? It was so difficult to climb the mountain with only a backpack with nothing but a little water and a few cookies inside that; he could not believe that such a mansion was made by human hands. Perhaps the ancient's stories about the participation of Satan were not unreasonable, because the stone mansion, in addition to being large, had a very scary and frightening appearance, which confirmed this belief. But in order to calm himself down, he thought that there must be another way that is more suitable for going, but no one knows that way. Perhaps over the past few centuries, rain and floods or mountain falls have damaged and destroyed the route. But why nothing had happened to the stone mansion. It therefore calls into question this argument. The more he researched this, the more he found nothing but contradictory information, which negated each other. The only way left was to climb the mountain and reach the mansion.

As he struggled to overcome his fears, he continued on his way. There was not much time left to disprove people's misconceptions about the existence of Satan and to show that ignorance is the greatest fear they have. He had been seriously researching the mansion for some time and had read many books. The existing mansion in front of him, although it looked scary and strange and there was no logic in its existence at this height, but still, its architectural signs indicated that human hands were involved in its construction and for some reason built it. The stone view, which from this distance was without any windows, looks more like a castle that the witches consider for themselves. At the top of the mansion was a tower several metres from the building and at the top of the tower was a strangely designed hatch that overlooked the city. The mansion is also covered with black and white stones, which attracted more attention. He was getting closer to it. He had to be more careful. From now on, more care was needed. Something special could happen at any moment. On the one hand, he had to be careful of city officials who were careful not to let anyone approach the mansion, and on the other hand, there were incidents that were waiting for him inside the mansion and could happen at any moment. He was almost in front of the mansion. He hid behind a large rock. In this way, he had the opportunity to rest a little and look around more calmly and monitor the situation. Everything seemed calm. He had passed through an area guarded by city officials. The only concern was what actually was waiting for him inside the mansion. He opened his bag. He took a bottle of water out of it and drank some of it. He could not wait long. Anyway, he had to return to the city before it got dark. He could not have done more than that. He closed the bottle and put it in the bag and got up. He decided to climb the boulder overlooking the mansion and look inside. The stone mansion was much larger than it looked. He looked around the mansion for the last time. No one was there. He climbed the rock slowly and reached the top very quickly. He raised his head cautiously to look inside the mansion. While out of horror and surprise, he could not breathe, and suddenly, he saw in front of him several people talking to each other. It was unbelievable to him. They were human, dressed in uniform and wearing white shawls. He could not even imagine such a thing in his imagination. A little further on, there was a hall with stone windows and thick curtains. But through one of the windows, he saw people holding a ceremony. Suddenly, fear took over his whole being. He could not stand there anymore. He had to get out of there as soon as possible before they could see him. But curiosity and what he saw inside the mansion made him decide to go a little further and at least try to see better inside the hall. There were a few pieces of stone next to him. He thought to himself that if he could step on them and climb the wall of the mansion, he could reach the back of a half-open window so that he could not be seen. To do this, he had to look at the corners of the mansion to make sure there was no guard. It was the same. There was no guard. Apparently, they knew so much about the people and were sure that no one had ever dared to climb the walls and look inside the Satan's Mansion, what the people called it.

He put his bag on the stone to prevent it from advancing, then reached the desired location. He walked slowly behind the window and stood in a semi-upright position. He raised his head cautiously and looked in through the corner of the window. Thirteen people were inside the hall. One was lecturing and twelve were sitting in double chairs. This made it easy to count them. All twelve wore black uniforms and hats of the same colour, with ten wearing white shawls and two wearing blue ones. The thirteenth person who was giving a speech was wearing a red shawl around his neck.

He tried to look more carefully into the hall. Some time passed like this. The two men, who were wearing blue shawls, got up and walked over to the lecturer, and the lecturer, who was calling someone by name, called each of the other ten, and with the help of those two, he gave them blue shawls to exchange with their white ones. As if it were a kind of graduation ceremony. Although he did not have the right angle of view and could not monitor everything well from this distance, he suddenly recognised with disbelief the faces of the two men wearing blue shawls. Yes, he was sure. Both were influential people in the city who had previously approached them for help and support to inspect the stone mansion, and they were not even willing to see and receive him. He was completely shocked. He could not easily leave and return. The matter had become more complicated, and the presence of the two had made the matter even stranger. Now that he has come here and made sure that there are no extra-terrestrial beings at work and that everything is manmade, he must understand why they came there. In fact, he who came there with such difficulty and from a dangerous path and under the sun, how was it possible that they were there with perfectly stylish and clean robes, without even being soiled. There must be a way and why they should come here at all and what was their intention from this gathering and why they did not inform the people about their presence, and on the other hand, they scared them. He tried to go a little further. Maybe he could identify other people as well. Suddenly, a rock slipped from under his feet and he fell down, clinging tightly to the closed window so that everyone in the hall and those standing in the yard could see him. He was so scared he could not go back to where he was. He hesitated for a moment. At that moment, a group in the hall ran to the window, opened it and violently dragged him into the hall. He was completely shocked. He was asked who he was and why he came there or who commissioned him. There was a controversy. Everyone was saying something until the man with the red shawl around his neck pointed to the two people standing next to him to take him away. He was completely scared. He did not know what to do. If he had a chance to escape, he would have done so, but he was sure he had to surrender to fate. At that moment, one of the most influential people in the city came forward and identified him and stared at him. Then he looked at the other person and said softly in his ear; then they took his hands and covered his face, carried him out of the hall with the lecturer. One of the attendees also signalled for the others to stay calm and avoid talking about it. Silence filled the hall again, and they left, and after passing through several dark corridors, moved to the door between the rocks. Then one of them pressed a key and the door opened and they entered the elevator and pressed the highest key on the floor. It was unbelievable that technology was at its best in this stone mansion. The elevator was one of them. By his condition and the severe pain he felt in his ankle, he made no attempt to escape, especially since he did not know which way out, and more importantly, his face was covered. He could only guess that he was inside a tower he had seen from the outside because he felt he had been inside the elevator for a long time. The elevator opened. They came out and moved a few steps. Then they spoke softly to someone who would let them in. The sound of opening came in the room and after a while the same sound again. As if they had been allowed to enter. They entered the room. Suddenly, they removed the cloth that had been thrown over his face. It was as if a man in white had allowed it. A tall, white-bearded man with a red shawl around his neck. He came towards him and turned around a little. His whole face turned white with terror. The man in white, who was called an architect, pointed to his secretary to get him some water. It was there that he realised that he was the architect who had built the stone mansion. They quickly gave him a glass of water. The architect indicated that he should be released to feel comfortable. They did the same. Then one of the most influential people in the city, who had identified him, came to the architect and spoke in his ear. Apparently, the man reported that he had come to them many times to inspect the mansion. He also took a glass of water to his mouth and examined the room under his eyes to give him a better chance to assess the situation. He could no longer hide his horror at seeing an official in the town square warn him against the law of not approaching the Satan's Mansion. Exactly the same official was sitting in a chair around the table in the corner of the room. But the person in charge did not know him. Moments passed like this, and he stared at the symbols inside the architect's room, which were on the table and on the walls. Then he noticed a hatch from which light shone into the room, illuminating the room, which was lit only by a small flame. Suddenly, he remembered the hatch at the top of the tower on the mansion and soon realised where he stood. The architect came to him. He had a smile on his face, then everyone except the person in charge left the room. Pointing to his foot, the architect noticed that he was injured and asked him to sit down. After a while, the architect started talking about himself and the stone mansion without talking about the reason for his presence. He pointed out that in this mansion, they are trying to create a framework with friendship and kindness in order to create a special order in the city with the help of the official and others. An order that was quite evident in the structure of the mansion and showed that the stone mansion was a good place for it. He continued that this is part of the activities of this mansion and the reason why they do not like to be seen is because people do not understand their activities properly. The architect believed that people did not have a correct understanding of the order that he and his companions had created for the people, and of course, he did not expect ordinary people and that everything he did was for the sake of the Creator and for the sake of their humanitarian nature. For this reason, they try to lead people to enlightenment and friendship and to bring them to what they deserve. This is done only in secret, and through those who are fully committed to it.

Little by little, fear and panic disappeared from his face. He felt better. Although he still did not know his own destiny. He tried to at least listen to the architect. Then the architect took his hand and helped him to get up and go to the hatch on the tower. Then he pointed out. He could see everything from there, the whole city. The architect continued: "Through this hatch, the whole city can be seen and well controlled. You can see that everything is going according to plan and there is nothing to worry about. So you do not have to risk it and come here." He paused for a moment. He also felt a little danger. He realised that he had come to a place where it might not be possible for him to leave and that these were just sentences to justify their actions and decisions. Fear took over his whole being again. He did not know what to do to convince the architect to forgive his sins. The architect looked at him and then went to the closet. He opened the door and from there took a white shawl and came to him and while putting it on his neck said:

> "Not everyone can become a member of the Stone Mansion, unless other members accept him and introduce him, and if he gets enough votes, he can become a member of the mansion. But there is only one way in which this process does not proceed, and that is when the architect decides to admit someone he has identified without formalities. You become a member of the stone mansion from now on and you cannot leave here until the architect decides. I hope you complete the next steps as well as possible. Congratulations."

Judge Violence

Judge Violence

"I have protest."

Suddenly, silence fell everywhere and eyes were drawn to the lawyer. Even from the defendant's point of view, it can be seen that he is surprised by his lawyer's reaction and is waiting to know what he is actually objecting to and how he wants to respond to the accusations levelled against him. However, he was not the only victim of violence that was charged with a crime and considered a criminal offense. Violence that was sometimes greater than the apparent crime. The judge looked at the lawyer powerfully and showed that there was no room for protest and that it was better for the lawyer to be a little patient so that the court could go through its main conditions. But the lawyer got up and announced in a louder voice for the second time:

> "I have protest. There is something that should be heard before any verdict is issued by you, dear judge of the court, which I am sure can prove the

innocence of the accused. Because, given the available evidence and the evidence that I will present, the course of the case will change."

This time, the glances of those present in court were met with curiosity. What was clear was the lawyer's remarks and the way he spoke, which caught everyone's attention and persuaded them to listen to his defence. Even the trial judge was no exception, and although he had been given sufficient time to defend himself and no longer had the right to do so, it was clear that the defence attorney knew when and with what sentences create a sense of curiosity to regain this right for himself and his client so that he can make the necessary impact on the final verdict at the right time.

The judge's excessive silence and constant glances indicated that the lawyer had been given the right to object so that there would be no room for doubt. Meanwhile, the defence attorney stood up with more courage as if he had been able to take part in a great battle and be its hero and then straightened his suit and then threw the papers in front of him over his glasses. He then looked at the audience and returned to the judge. His professional conduct showed that he was completely in control of what he was doing and had no doubts about it and that he could change the situation in favour of the accused, who had been silent for a few minutes. After hearing the word of protest, the accused seemed to be alive again. In fact, when he reviewed his circumstances and charges, he never thought that these cases would be considered a crime at all, let alone a heavy sentence awaited him. In fact, when he learned of his charges and the legal status, he was more surprised than worried about the future of the trial and did not think that such matters would be considered a crime and that he would have such heavy sentences. There was no correlation between the conviction and the crime that took place. He had full hope for the voice that had now declared in the hall with authority that I was protesting, and he hoped that, at least if it did not affect the course of the meeting, some of his heart's words would be uttered, and perhaps help the audience from misled. He even hoped that if there was no way out for him, he would at least be a victim so that future generations would learn from his conviction and not treat other people like that again.

Before continuing his speech, the defence attorney looked at the defendant briefly to see the effects of his behaviour. At that moment, the defendant's anxious looks told him that he was waiting to see his lawyer try to support him, although he seemed to have no hope. The defence attorney then turned to the judge in the same manner and continued without waiting to be allowed to speak:

> "In the current situation, my client has faced accusations that in fact, in today's social conditions, these issues are part of the personal rights and citizenship of individuals. You may say that I said this at the beginning of my defence, but I want to know how someone can be convicted of charges, all of which are considered a subset of behavioural violence, while the sentence is much more violent than what can be controlled. It is considered violence. However, the list of charges against my client is still under discussion. But even

if these charges are accepted, there is still no convincing reason for such verdicts. How is it possible for a person to engage in behavioural violence that is several times more violent than his or her behaviour? This means that we ourselves are promoting violence in the justice system. This is a question that I ask you, dear judge and attendees, not only to defend my client but also as someone who has worked in this field for many years. I have been to several court meetings so far, and every time after the meeting is over and a verdict is issued, I ask myself that in order to save society from social violence, instead of seeking an appropriate solution, it has promised the defendants much more horrific violence, to keep them from committing any crime. However, my discussion here is general, and I will object to each of the cases attributed to my client and I will provide a full explanation of all the cases."

He assessed the situation by looking shrewdly at the judge, who had lowered his head and flipped the papers in front of him. The silence that prevailed in the courtroom seemed to create the conditions for the individual to read out the charges and to defend them, and this groundwork, which was suddenly accompanied by his protest, seemed more effective. Because if he had made these remarks at the legal time, he might not have had the ground for such a speech, which he now created as a monologue and spoke as a ruler in the courtroom. Rather than being a lawyer, he was a skilled speaker who knew the psychology of individuals well. So he looked at the papers in front of him, and after moving them, he chose one and placed it in front of him, pretending that he wanted to read it, and that it would be better for everyone present to remain silent and listen to what he had to say.

"First one: You are accused of disrespecting social rules, given the repeated warnings, you live as a threat in today's society. According to the existing laws, you have been sexually abused and have not married at the appointed time, and this shows that if a person lives alone, it will definitely cause harm to himself and society and cause sexual annoyance, at least for himself. In such cases, it has been proven that this issue can have many consequences. Such behaviours are referred to as sexual violence in the law, and whoever carries this violence with them indicates that this person is not trustworthy, and that someone who engages in violent behaviour has the ability to do so in society. Assuming this to be true, how does a judge, instead of providing a good platform for resolving such problems, classify these issues as behavioural violence and instead issue a verdict to the defendant that is several times more violent than what is nothing has happened yet. It seems that society tends to threaten its citizens to cross a path that some believe is the only possible way to salvation. I must state here that my client, because of the physical and mental condition, he suffered as a result of the loss of his ex-wife, still does not see the conditions to return to a normal life and normal social routine. Of course, I hope you keep in mind that this can be a threat to his next life, which, of course, is violence for others. This self-sacrificing behaviour of my client is itself a sign of humanity and a proper social understanding."

He looked at his client again. A short smile was etched on his lips. It was as if it was his voice coming out of the lawyer's mouth. It was as if he knew him well and understood all the threats to his life. His smile was so short that no one but his lawyer could recognise it. The accused, who had been cold all his life until a few moments ago, was feeling a little comfortable and relaxed. The court's initial ruling was such that it could affect his entire future and keep him in silence. Fear of it made him completely speechless and unable to utter a word even in self-defence. The meeting he had with his lawyer yesterday was held in silence, and if the lawyer's courage and experience had not been accompanied on the day of the court, the meeting would have ended now and he would have had to accept the violence that society has chosen for him. The court condemned him for accepting it. However, he was not yet optimistic about the success of his lawyer. He was only happy that he was saying things that his closed lips could not say, and he saw that even if he lost the meeting, he was still pleased that a part of his speech reached the audience. Attendees, who seemed to be just like socially enacted laws, had a passion for violence, and at the end of the session, they might have been looking for something to complete their show today and make their newspaper headlines prosperous. Even in the eyes of some of them, there was a flash of joy.

They were excited to be present in the courtroom to witness the execution of another of their citizens, without thinking that they themselves will be the next victims and no one knows or wants to take action to change this situation.

> "As for the second case, you are accused of not following the rules and frameworks in your administrative system and your job as an employee and sometimes causing chaos and disorder. The statistics and administrative correspondence received from your managers show that you have doubts about the applicable registered laws and have spoken about the realisation of the right. But you should know that in society, if anyone wants to express their opinion, the existing order is endangered and may cause chaos. These things are explained to the employees before hiring, and you should know that you are not in a position to disturb the atmosphere in the community and cause disorder. And as the defence attorney of the accused, I would like to ask you, Honourable Judge, if in an office or any company or organisation, people as managers are abusing their management conditions and circumventing the rules, is it appropriate for the employees to remain silent and in any conditions to work? Is it not the right of them to be able to object legally when they feel that a person's right is being violated? It has been seen again and again in today's society that general managers abuse their current position and conditions and continue to be monotonous if there is no protest from such people.

Now you think that the violent behaviour of some managers is questionable or a protest that an employee has verbally and respectfully towards his working conditions. Isn't it better to give enough space to criticism and suggestions of employees and citizens so that they can comment on their social situation and its improvement at the right time and in the right situations? I think in a society where a respected judge sits in a position and warns people against existing violence, and the reason for my client's accusations in this case is precisely social violence, he certainly pays attention to the issue of defending civil rights and constructive criticism and suggestions. It can be effective in improving the current situation."

This was the first time the judge had looked away from the papers and looked at the defence attorney and the defendant. His face looked a little calmer, and his gaze was kind. He overthrew the defendant, who was completely desperate and at the same time checked the feedback of the defence attorney's speech in the presence of those present. It seemed that the defence attorney was quite successful in changing the direction of the court and was able to attract the attention of the audience. So in order to read the third case, he flattened his chest to actually allow himself to start talking again. It even seemed that the trial judge had deliberately given him permission to dissuade him from giving a sentence he did not want to give. In any case, the verdict depended on the good defence of the accused and his lawyer so that he could influence the confession of those present and include his pardon. In any case, since he did not have a private plaintiff and whatever he was, it was due to non-compliance with social and civil laws, so it was possible for the judge to even write and pardon the accused. But fear of public opinion may have gripped the judge, who could not state his true decision. The lawyer turned to the papers, assuming that he had been able to align the judge with himself and continued:

"Third one: You are accused of having suspicious interactions with people who are prohibited by law or have a record. It is even recorded in the available documents that you have met and stood up with them on several occasions and attended their parties. This means that you are not afraid of what society has provided for you to stay away from potential threats, and you are ready for any expression of violence against society. But in my opinion, dear Judge, these people you mentioned are the ones who have been repeatedly abused by the society and have now returned to the heart of the society. Perhaps this is a sign of civil violence that ignores these people. These people, referred to as suspects, need social interaction. When they can be present in society freely and after serving their sentence, then they also have the right to communicate with others as before and not to be ignored. This shows the right attitude of my client, who, with self-sacrifice, prepares the conditions so that the prevailing violence does not affect these people any more, and they see themselves on the verge of a new social life."

For the first time in this period, the judge's smile showed that he was satisfied with the defence attorney's way of defending and wanted him to continue in this way. But because some of those present were sitting in front of him with grim faces, waiting for the judge's initial verdict to be carried out and to watch a spectacular display of modern violence in front of them, the judge quickly changed his smile as he showed that he did not smile at all and even went a step further and frowned a little. But because the lawyer was smarter than he seemed, he shook his head and said:

"Fourth one: You not only do not actively participate in the ceremonies and extracurricular that the society considers for the citizens but sometimes you refuse to participate in them."

At that moment, the voice of those present in the meeting was raised. It seemed that this was a sufficient reason for the trial of the accused and showed that they may have ignored the previous cases, but the judge should have reacted strongly to this case and tried to persuade the judge by making noise and commotion. So as not to reconsider their verdict and make the space in a way that agrees with them. However, this behaviour did not go unanswered, and a group started making noise at the request of the accused. This was the first time that the defendant found out that a group in the courtroom was in his favour and had come to support him. But the atmosphere in the

93

courtroom was so hostile that they could not be heard, and when the defence attorney began his unusual speech, they realised that they might have the courage to protest and defend the accused. Meanwhile, the judge knocked on the table and invited everyone to be silent, pointing to the lawyer with an authoritative look to finish his speech sooner. The lawyer, who did not want to lose the situation he had reached with difficulty, immediately continued:

"Dear Judge, as you are aware, some issues are considered as personal conditions of individuals and their presence or absence is optional according to the law. If someone does not attend a ceremony, there is no reason to reject that gathering, but perhaps the conditions for attending it are not ready for him. In addition, these ceremonies and extracurricular activities have been announced in accordance with the law. How is it possible that some voluntary matters have changed colour over the course of time and become mandatory? Perhaps the protesters in the hall should take a closer look at the rules and avoid such reactions. This is something that my client is aware of and has tried to use the rules and its optionality in his own way and to avoid participating in these meetings until he is ready to attend. My client's interference in the voluntary affairs may be a kind of behavioural and emotional violence to others that threatens him to attend a ceremony without any real desire to do so and to diminish the quality of that gathering."

The lawyer, who had missed the pulse of the speech a few minutes before, did not want it to happen again, so he continued immediately and without pausing:

> "Fifth one: It has been announced that my client does not use TV and other means of communication in his apartment, which means that he wants to protest against the programs. Dear Judge, my client spends his favourite time in a way that he does not have enough time for social programs. In meetings with my client, I have stated that they have limited free time to study and that they are not interested in pursuing some of the programs, which in fact provide a list of several that are nothing more than violence education. It may be better for the citizen to choose their own times and entertainments, just remember it does not harm others."

The lawyer knew full well that he did not have much time left and that he should read and defend the remaining two charges as soon as possible, as this was the last chance he could use to save his client. He glanced at his watch and decided to finish his speech in the next few minutes, not to allow the prolongation to have a negative effect on the judge and those present at the meeting.

> "Sixth one: Some of the existing gatherings are accompanied by physical and verbal violence, and my client has avoided attending them. In this case, it is stated that the accused, although he should be committed to the works and national unity, but he is not diligent in this regard and it causes lack of

solidarity in the society. But, dear Judge, as I said, my client avoids the framework violence of the society, and this does not mean that he does not believe in the authority of the society, but he is one of the citizens who strongly believes in unity, and he himself said it explicitly."

The judge bit his lip and shook his head as if in conflict, pointing out that the last case should be read as soon as possible so that he could issue a final verdict. The defendant seemed quite pleased this time and was satisfied that his lawyer had authoritatively taken over the audience. Now he felt a little comfortable and hoped for the end of the defence.

"But the last case: the accused does not pay attention to the timely payment of duties and taxes announced by the government. Since these sums are only to improve the conditions of citizenship, the lack of participation of individuals causes confusion in the governing affairs and order in the society. Dear Judge, this is absolutely true, but I must say that citizens sometimes have problems in their social affairs, such as illness, accident, or mistake, and this has a direct impact on their payment terms. But since these people are citizens of the same society, they should be given the opportunity to regain their financial stability and return to their former ways. My client never intends to run away from the job entrusted to him, and he will pay the full amount specified, and he can offer his personal apartment to provide a guarantee."

Silence filled the hall. A few moments later, the defence attorney continued:

"Thank you for the time given to me and my client. I hope I have been able to prevent possible violence that threatens others, especially my client, with my remarks and to make it clear that any sentence can be far more violent than the client. I am accused of it, and it is better to think of appropriate solutions to save our citizens instead of threatening behaviours."

The defendant looked at the lawyer as a sign of gratitude and thanked him with a smile while tears were flowing from his eyes. The lawyer also gave him hope by shaking his head and smiling deeply. The noise of the audience filled the whole hall. This time, the judge allowed the voices to continue so that he could have enough time to think and give order. This sentence was final and there was no opportunity to change it. Therefore, all aspects had to be considered when issuing it.

Shortly afterwards, the judge knocked on the table and invited everyone to remain silent.

"You heard the lawyer. According to this verdict, the defendant will be pardoned from all seven charges, so that we may be the primary link in order to prevent violence that threatens the defendants and is chained together

The Sanctuary of the Temple

The Sanctuary of the Temple

The seventh day passed while the monk was imprisoned in a room inside the temple and no one was allowed to attend. This was exactly what he had said before he entered the temple, and no one knew how long it would last. Each of the monks commented on this, sometimes contradictory opinions were expressed. But this was the result of a meeting that took place seven days ago, and in that meeting where the other monks of the temple were present, the senior monk declared that the only way to save the temple was to deal with it himself, so that he could solve this big problem before it became too late. Many solutions had been taken in this regard. But none of them was able to return the temple to its original position, as if the need was shown to sacrifice the highest authority of the temple in this way. Many monks at the meeting, however, disagreed. But the position of the senior monk was such that they could not dissuade him from doing so. In fact, this was against the rules of the temple. Although the issues were followed up through meetings, it was ultimately the senior monk who had to make the final decision and announce it. Some even thought that this might be the last thing they could do. In fact, the meeting held in the assembly hall of the temple, which was attended by other monks, was because the senior monk intended to officially declare the condition of the temple to be acute and to warn them of the need for salvation. Of course, this issue had been discussed for months and everyone was aware of it. But the way the senior monk had chosen to resolve the issue was indigestible to them. Perhaps at first they did not believe in the senior monk and thought that this method and failure to achieve the desired result, could make the situation worse and worse than it is. But the resolute and decisive face of the senior monk prevented them from protesting and did not allow doubt to be expressed in their hearts and to discourage him from doing so. On the other hand, the senior monk seemed to be aware of what was going on in the monks' minds. He then asked them not to let other people know until the final result was reached, as he could not even determine the estimated time that could guarantee the temple's prosperity. In this way, they could control the behaviour of the people in this regard and defend the credibility of the temple against them.

In fact, the main cause of all the worries was the people who quickly moved away from the temple and sometimes even saw it as contrary to their wishes. The senior monk, who had not been elected to this position for a long time, had announced that he intended to lead the people to the temple, and this and the solutions he proposed were the main reasons for his election, even he was so young. He spoke so decisively, with a penetrating word and a special and determined passion on the day of his election, that other monks saw him as a saviour who was to not only revitalise the temple but to influence their lives and re-establish them as a leader among the people and became popular again. During these years, the linear and uniform movement of the temple had caused people to distance themselves from it and consider its affairs as merely as a ritual that they can leave aside whenever they want and take care of their own affairs. Circumstances showed that perhaps the senior monk himself was a great help, because he was younger than others and understand people better. Even strict laws could not restore the monks to their former position. The situation was probably such that soon the main hall of the temple, which was a place of worship for the people, no longer saw anyone but a few of its monks, and this situation was considered a crisis for the temple. In a short time, several senior monks were elected and dismissed, but none of them were able to attract the attention of the people again, and there was even a whisper among the monks that the senior monk could be considered as the last bullet, and if he could not solve this problem, they must definitely join the people to save themselves from the possible harms that threaten them. This was an indication of a lack of faith in the temple and the senior monk, which he had made clear on the day of the meeting, and the reason he was acting alone was the lack of confidence in other monks, who were no longer aware of what they did it in the temple; even they did not have faith, and they also looked at their clothes as a way of earning a living, not as servants who served the temple. Even the senior monk had announced in the meeting that everything was out of his way and that it might be necessary for a hero to come and change everything, even if this hero was sacrificed in this way. To the astonishment of the other monks, they preferred to remain silent so that new decisions of which they knew nothing would cause them trouble. But in the meantime, two people announced that they wanted to walk this path with the senior monk. Although everyone tried to confirm him, the two specifically asked the senior monk to follow him as he wished. The senior monk, in order to ease everyone's mind, rose from behind the conference table and announced that this issue is done completely individually and it is better that no one interferes. But because he was not sure how long he would be inside the room, from the first day of his election, he entrusted matters to another monk, who had a special place among the others, and instructed him not only to take care of the affairs of the temple but do not let anyone disturb his privacy inside the worship room and in the sanctuary of the temple, for which he was no more than a prisoner, even if he spends a long time in that room without food and water. They do not even need to check his physical condition after any time he has been in the room because he was confident that he could do so and he was ready and healthy in every way and showed that nothing could stop him. In this regard. The monk, as if from the very first day of the election of the senior monk, considered himself as the highest official of the temple, respectfully observed his orders and perhaps prepared himself to succeed him. This was the pain that the senior monk thought about, and he knew that as long as the monks thought so in their moral affairs, they could not invite people to the temple. Considering that he was fully aware of what was going on in his successor's mind, he looked at the monks for the last time, said goodbye to them and went to the exit of the meeting hall.

When he entered the meeting hall, silence and darkness filled the whole space and he did not see anyone there for worship. He only saw the servants cleaning the temple, and he heard the sound of hymns being played in the temple. With tears in his eyes, he looked at the empty chairs and, hoping to see countless people on them soon, walked up the stairs to the balcony. He once again examined the condition of the temple from the balcony and then proceeded with more confidence and determination than ever to the sanctuary of the temple, which was built and considered in the quietest place of the temple and was considered a place of worship. He stood in front of the entrance. He waved at a few people who had hurriedly escorted him there, then entered the sanctuary of the temple and closed the door behind him. The monks kept talking to each other about this and did not know what the end would be. On the other hand, each of the twelve monks inside the temple considered it their duty not to talk about this incident and to keep it a secret in order to prevent the temple's reputation from being damaged, because if people knew about it, it would be a way to ridicule them and paved the way for the final destruction of the temple. They did not even know what to say or react in response to those who wanted to see the senior monk. Even during this week, they not only did not try to attract more people but sometimes escaped from their questions and tried not to get involved in issues that might one day be affected by any of their orientations. Even the monks had come to the conclusion that it was better to put some kind of conservatism in their path, because none of them knew about their future, and this showed well that the temple was alone and rejected even from within, and its companions were nothing but some to work there and they have no other view on it. This was the same pain that the senior monk had experienced, knowing that the temple would not really be expected of ordinary people without support from within, as long as the members themselves did not believe in what they were doing. He believed that people were intelligent and could not rely on what its custodians themselves did not believe in. So the senior monk, considering these circumstances, considered the only available solution to be his own devotion, even if he is imprisoned inside the worship room for many years and his voice is not heard, although he had prepared himself for all the consequences. Suddenly, the door opened and in disbelief an old and weak man with a crooked back and a stressed face appeared on the doorstep. One of the servants, whose turn it was to guard in front of the worship room, saw this scene and shouted for help. The servant's voice rang out inside the main hall of the temple like an alarm bell, gathering the monks in the temple with the other servants. It was utterly impossible for everyone to believe that he had seen in front of him a man who had been so cheerful last week and had been elected as one of the youngest senior monks, as if he had been seen in front of his room for forty years. And if they did not know that he was the senior monk who went into solitude, and if they did not know his standing posture and movements, they would never have been able to identify him. Everyone stood in front of the door in shock and anxiety, as if ready to flee in time of need, watching the situation. Everyone was waiting to see what awaited them. At the same time, the senior monk, pointing to the number of monks with his eyes, waved to come to his aid and save him from falling. Two servants approached him very carefully and hesitantly, took him by the armpits, took him to the next room and placed him on the couch. Another servant who had just come to his senses dispelled the fear of what he had seen and brought a bottle of water for the senior monk to drink. No one knew what had happened inside the sanctuary, but whatever it was, it had suddenly made the senior monk forty years older and now thinking about his death. They closed the sanctuary by the order of the monk's successor too quickly to investigate and find out what happened inside the room and why the monk appeared in front of them in this way. They quickly emptied the room where the senior monk was lying on the couch, and all but his successor and one of the monks were thrown out of the room. The senior monk, who was breathing hard, drank some water and then looked at both of them, swallowing his saliva as if he had come a long way and said that he was carrying good news, pointing to his successor. He announced that the other monks had come into the room so that he could tell them everything he had in mind at once. Although this was not a pleasant matter for the successor, as he did not see the conditions conducive to competition, he acted quickly and opened the door of the room and pointed to one of the servants to bring the other monks there very soon.

It was not long before the twelve monks sat next to the senior monk, waiting for him to learn what had happened inside the sanctuary. The senior monk moved on the couch with the help of a monk and then, with a twinkle in his eyes for success, said with a triumphant smile, "From now on, for seven days, as long as I was inside the temple sanctuary, people can come to the temple and recite their wishes. From the moment they come to the temple and ask for what they want, they will get everything they want. Thus, I feel that perhaps this declaration of need will cause people to return to their ancient temple and place of worship. This is all that inspired me and took away all my youth. You can tell people as soon as possible so you don't waste time, because this can be necessary and vital for many."

Soon the noise in the temple assembly hall was muffled. A large crowd had gathered there, each praying. Many people were standing outside the temple, waiting for a few people to come out and make room for them to ask for their wishes from the temple. With each passing moment, the excitement among the people increased. A new group had received the news, and they seemed very upset that they had been left out. The city was completely closed. Although initially considered a joke, the feedback from those who came to the temple and got what they wanted caused the news to reach the whole city much sooner than they thought. Everywhere in the city, there was talk of a senior monk and how the temple was the main point of salvation for them. Some regretted staying away from the temple and not coming there during this time. Some people thought of nothing but getting to the meeting hall. Little by little, the excitement and joy of their presence became an anomaly, and a group of people sat in the waiting line protesting why a city of this size should have only one temple. Little by little, the big joke turned into a special catastrophe, and the senior monk looked at the people on the chair from the balcony in a weak state and seemed satisfied and happy with what was in front of him. To prevent chaos and possible clashes, a meeting was held on the second day for the monks to make decisions in this regard. The only solution was to give each person only a limited amount of time so that all the people could get to the meeting hall. But managing the countless population of the entire city was almost impossible without sufficient manpower and guiding them was not an easy task. Tensions between people outside the temple in several-kilometre queues in the darkest hours of the night were inevitable, and the city's security forces, despite their best efforts, did not see the power to bring order to the riot. This situation reached its peak when the last days were approaching and only a few percent of the people of the whole city were able to get inside the temple hall. Consecutive meetings of city officials and even monks were not effective, and the senior monk, who had been in eternal silence since that day, did not help. The city was almost drawn into an unwanted controversy that aroused the violence of the people and prepared them to do anything to achieve their goal. By the end of the fifth day, even the whole country was on alert. Violence to get to the meeting hall in some parts of the city caused bloodshed and strife, and people, regardless of whether they were men or women or even their family members, only thought that they should not miss the last two days. On the sixth day, news reached the temple that there had been heavy fighting around the temple and that all the people in groups were being added to the fighting. The controversy, which continued, reached its peak on the seventh day, when even the security forces and the government considered themselves worthy to enter the temple. The crowd inside the temple was so large that people trampled on each other and many suffocated inside the temple. On the other hand, there was a great battle outside the temple, and no matter what they came to the temple for, bloodshed continued. People were each fighting to save themselves from the current situation, and the more helpless were crushed under the feet of others. The darkness had contributed to this and had brought the temple, which was lit by the light of the candles, into complete darkness, since no one could replace the candles. The shouts of the people who were dying inside or being killed outside the temple filled the whole city. Meanwhile, the senior monk, who had become motionless and lifeless as a body, stared at them with wide, dry eyes and smiled at what had made the temple stand out and immortalise it.

Blue Dahila

Blue Dahlia[*]

"If I came to see you today, it does not mean that I lost my self-esteem, but I thought that you could help me. This is exactly the reason for my request; I saw you in a way that others might not see. In my opinion, you are someone who can be trusted and there will definitely be no abuse. A character who shows a person who deserves any trust and leaves no room for concern. I'm sure you will help me. I have never heard from anyone that you have disappointed the person who came. Of course, I know this is very different from other people's issues, but in general, what is the difference? The important thing is that there is a need. I feel good that you are sitting so patiently and listening to me, and I hope to see your positive response. You think

---

[*]**Blue Dahlia:** *It often has a different meaning, which is a sign of elegance, inner strength, creativity, change and dignity. It also refers to all those who adhere to their sacred values.*

you are helping someone in need. I think if you look at it this way, the problem will be solved. I know that you are a person who moves within your moral framework. But know that rejecting this request is not only a sign of immorality but quite the opposite, it proves that you are not attached to anyone or anything. It is too childish to ignore individual needs, as it may lead to immorality. Do not think that I feel good sitting here in front of you and I am happy to beg you in this way. But man cannot understand another man until there is a need in him. I urge you to look a little deeper. What is the fault of people like me who have to live in such conditions? We also have rights. We like to enjoy our lives. Now that such possibilities do not exist, there is no reason for us to leave our needs. It does not matter to me or to others like me whether this is right or wrong. We lived long enough as nuns. Except how long a person lives, which should be like this throughout her life. Please consider my request only once. You may be wondering why I chose you for this job. You want to know the cause. Because I'm sure you have a special commitment to ethics and I can easily give myself to you, and I know that after that everything will be forgotten. This is exactly where you can test and enjoy your ethics. Do not forget that whatever is presented to you as an ethical framework can take another form. What is clear is that there are people in need like me for whom you are responsible."

Time and time again, he heard words like responsibility and ethics and pondered them in his mind. He had never looked at it the way she talked about it. He was happy that he felt safe in his life. But on the other hand, he could not be indifferent to the needs of others. However, if he answered in the affirmative, he was credited with mental and physical debauchery. But he himself was aware that he was not looking for any particular pleasure, and he was upset that for social reasons he could not meet her needs. Doing so could never do him any harm, but deep down, he did not feel good. He found himself in a quagmire, losing on every side he moved. He did not even imagine that he could pursue moral effects in doing immoral things. He was frustrated that he was at a crossroads where he could not choose the right path. He got up from his chair. He looked at his watch. There was not much time left. Repeated requests and insistences led him to accept the appointment. Although it was not to his liking, he considered himself responsible for the needs of others. According to his intellectual structures, there was no contradiction, but his only problem was the way society views such people. It was quite a mess and the stress had taken over his whole being. He liked to shout and say that if she is here, it is only because he wants to help a fellow human being and it has nothing to do with enjoyment. He insisted that he at least control himself and be satisfied with what he wanted to do. But he was so upset that he could not concentrate. As he was ready, he went to the side of the bed and threw himself on it and slowly began to count the flowers of wallpaper next to him, which were mixed together.

He knew he was just wasting time doing this and had not taken any positive steps to calm himself down. This was the only option available for relaxation, even if it did not work. He was upset that the wallpaper was full of blue dahlia flowers. He was always very sensitive to this flower and if his wife allowed it, he would change it at the earliest opportunity. The flowers were so tangled that his eyes went black and sometimes made him feel heavy on his eyelids. He no longer wanted to resist and wanted to go to a deep sleep and enjoy it and forget about the blue dahlia of wallpaper. Maybe his presence there and what he was waiting for were all just a deep sleep. Maybe he was still asleep and thought he was awake. He would definitely wake up now and see that his wife had greeted him with a cup of coffee.

In order to keep his wife away from him, it was enough to say that she would go to her family home for a few days, and she would definitely accept it without any hesitation. He was satisfied that there were no lies in their lives, and this was probably the first time he had experienced the condition of lying. But he fights with himself that he has not lied and there is no shame. He just wants to help someone in need. But he was sure that no one trusted his honesty in this particular matter, even though everyone considered him an honest man. He did not feel good that people could not understand what he understood. The main halfway had already passed. There was no opportunity to return. He should not have accepted it, but he had accepted. It was better not to think about it anymore and to focus on the fact that he did it for the satisfaction of a human being. However, he has made decisions in this direction that have not been to his desire.

The bell rang. He quickly looked at his watch. The time had come. She had even arrived a few minutes earlier. If she was only a few minutes late, he could have excused himself for waiting for her and leaving after the deadline. But it was not a good excuse. He felt weak because his inner mood was changing at every moment and he could not reach a fixed result. He tried to get out of bed with the same feeling, but it seemed like a difficult task. He still could not forget the blue dahlia flowers on the wallpaper. This made him more nervous. He got up and went to the door. He looked out through the peephole. Various and beautiful colours danced before his eyes, and his resistance to what he had been taught against the waves of colourful dancing was fruitless. He even thought about it for a moment, now that he was about to sink into sin, to enjoy it, though he was convinced that his presence was to help someone who had come to his office several times last week and begged him for the need to be considered, which is inherent in all beings and must be satisfied. He blamed himself for wasting so much time knowing it was a natural thing to do. Convinced that he might later regret what he was doing, he quickly opened the door.

When the door opened, he forgot all that he had been afraid of during this time, and he felt a sense of satisfaction, thinking that what they had said might not always be true. He was very happy that all his doubts were gone and he was ready to do what he wanted to do. He no longer wanted to think about anything and saw this as the reward of the pure intention of his heart that was given to him, and if he feels himself in heaven, it is all because he has never had an instinct and has looked at it logically. Now, the universe had the answer to his goodness in front of him. All of this passed quickly in front of his eyes, and, assuming that no action would go unanswered, he invited her into his apartment. Before closing the door, he looked outside for safety. From last week until now, he was not calm and had so many different types of mental conflict, but now, he had a pleasant feeling and was relax like someone who had reached the shore after a week of sea turbulence. For a moment, he found himself worthy of all these pleasures, and it was this motivation that gave him a sense of calm because of the decision he had made. Even looking at the guest in his apartment, he thought that he could still help her and that it might be a mistake to have a limit. He was no longer afraid to enjoy this relationship, and with this logic, he came to justify that every good deed deserves a reward, and this is the reward that has been considered, and there is no need to worry anymore. He no longer even thought about his wife lying to her or betraying her. In fact, from the point of view of this act, it is no longer considered betrayal, and lying is also expedient, and in fact, he has not committed any sin that he wants to escape from.

The colours were moving in front of his eyes, and he was dazzled. But why, no matter how focused he was, he could not forget the blue dahlia flowers and estimate the number of colourful wallpaper flowers next to his bed. Perhaps colours were the main cause of his mistakes. The mistakes that were already in his eyes and did not allow him to realise the truth. He rubbed his eyes lightly with his hands. They faded a little, but when they returned to normal, he saw the situation as before. Nothing had changed, and he was still waiting for someone who had repeatedly asked him several times last week to help her with a moral mindset to satisfy one of her emotionally rooted needs. He had a special life in which the slogan of morality always waved. At first, he objected, but then, since he considered himself responsible for the peace and happiness of others in life, he agreed to help her only once so that she too could feel the taste of pleasure in her being. Perhaps he saw himself as so great that he could help someone on earth without asking for anything in return. Finally, in her last request, he found himself obliged to do so, although he was not satisfied with the depth of his being. The bell rang. He looked at his watch. There were a few minutes left. He could no longer doubt his decision. There was no time for doubt. It was better not to think about anything anymore and to respect what is destined for it. Maybe he should have given up from the beginning and not had so much tension with himself. Maybe he was taking it too seriously, and it did not contradict moral principles. This is what has existed in all beings since the beginning of creation. So it was better not to think about anything anymore and to open the door and accept what was waiting for him with open arms. He got up and went to the door. From the peephole, he examined the outside. He expected to have in front of his eyes what he had encountered in his dream. But no one was behind the door. He was a little more careful. But he did not see anyone. Fear took over. Maybe it was his wife who came back and found out. But it was a futile thought because he had called her before he laid on the bed and was sure he was at least a day away from getting there. He waited a while. He wanted to wait, maybe the doorbell would ring again. He even thought that there was no ringing at all and that he might be imaginary again. It was only a few minutes ago that he saw her in his dream inside the apartment, and he was so excited that he thought the doorbell rang. But what was the cause of all this fear and panic? He has not yet made a mistake. He even thought that this was done simply because of his sense of humanity. He opened the apartment involuntarily. He could not stand it anymore. He wanted to know what had happened. He was sure he had heard the bell. The door opened. No one was outside. He looked to the end of the corridor. He turned and returned to the apartment in surprise. Suddenly, he noticed a piece of paper pasted on the door. He glanced. It was more like a note. He removed it from the door. In disbelief, he realised that he had heard the bell correctly and that this note was written by her in an unbalanced handwriting with trembling hands.

> "I came here. I doubted because I was not sure what I was doing. You were right. Thank you for agreeing to help me. I'm sorry if I informed you late."

He came into the apartment. He looked around. He looked at the neat and stylish clothes he was wearing. He had never worn these clothes before. He went to his bed and threw himself on it. A bitter smile settled on his lips. His whole being seemed to have been questioned. Tears welled up in his eyes. He got up. While holding the letter, he decided to greet his wife next week in his new clothes.

Holy Orb

Holy Orb*

He went to the entrance of the building to make sure it was closed and carefully inspected the windows one by one. The sound of the wind could be heard through the windows, doubling his anxiety and worry. It was raining heavily, and this isolated him the most and did not allow him to leave his building and save himself from the scary conditions. Of course, he had nowhere to go at night, but he could still go to a friend's house and save himself from the illusion he had, although he thought that maybe it was not an illusion and that night was really threatening him. He lived alone for a long time but rarely did he get anxious, although he knew the root of it well and in fact he saw himself as the cause of these mental states. If he had paid a little more attention to his speech or not dared to show such unbalanced behaviour,

---

***Holy Orb and Cross** is a sphere on which a cross is placed. Since the Middle Ages, this has been a symbol of the authority of the church and is depicted on coins and in iconography with a royal sceptre. The Cross on the Orb refers to Jesus' dominion over the entire earth, holding the earth in his hands as a leader.

that rainy night inside his building could certainly have been one of the best nights of his life. But now that he was paying attention, he saw that not only was the sound of the rain not as pleasant as usual but that he did not have the capacity to hear the angry rain hit the window panes, and in fact, it made him nervous. Involuntarily, he put his hands to his ears and held them tightly to prevent the sound reflected inside him. He felt calm for a few moments, so he decided to go to the bedroom earlier and sleep before the fear took over to accompany him until morning. He looked at his watch. It was a long time before midnight. He preferred to drink a hot drink before going to bed to control both himself and the cold. He picked up the kettle by the fire and filled his glass, listening to the sounds around him at the same time to keep everything under control. So he stood in front of the fireplace and stared at it. He could clearly see how the Holy Orb burned in the fire without being harmed. He certainly had gone too far and did not need to do so to prove his point. But perhaps the presence of others in the cafe had increased his excitement. He could still hear his uttering loudly among the others and how he had gone to the Holy Orb and thrown it into the fire in the cafe's fireplace. By doing so, he insulted the beliefs of others in the least possible way, which seemed unlikely to him, who considered himself a free-thinking man. Now, in addition to fear and panic, a sense of stupidity has been added to his feelings about how he can step into such places again, while not being bothered by the heavy gazes of the people of the city. He became conspicuous. There was certainly no need to question the beliefs of others. His friends also provoked him too much. Although he believed that there were no holies and that it was only the human

120

needy mind that sought a higher power, its current mood had a different meaning, especially when a friend warned him of the consequences. At that moment, the answer he thought was appropriate was his laughter, which was more like a laugh to make fun of. He drank some more of his drink and tried to show that these issues did not interfere with his horror and that they were just the product of his imagination. A bitter smile settled on his lips. He was sure he was sceptical, but he refused to admit it and even speak in private. He heard little sounds. It was as if there were other people in the house besides him. He went to the desk drawer by the window, pulled it out, took out a flashlight and immediately opened the cupboard and picked up his hunting gun. He felt safe holding a gun and a flashlight. But that was not enough. He could feel the presence of other creatures around him. He had to visit all the rooms to make sure that he was delusional and that no one but himself was at home. It started from there. He took his gun and visited the only room on the ground floor. There was nothing but absolute darkness and then light that illuminated the room. He came out of the room and looked at the stairs. The bedrooms were on the top floor of the building and he had to visit them as well. Although his own bedroom was there. There was really no need to have such a large building. He visited the living room for the last time and climbed the stairs. He put the flashlight in his pocket and turned on the light switch very quickly. First, he went to the next bedroom and then to his own bedroom. He examined everything carefully. He even looked inside the closets. He bent down and looked under the bed. He also reached for the clothes hanging in his closet. Everything seemed normal except for the eerie noises that whispered in his ear, promising him a dangerous night. He was completely desperate and did not know how to spend that night. He turned off the lights behind him. He took a deep breath and pretended that he was fine and that he needed to rest, and he seemed to go to bed earlier so that his nightmares might end. He went to the bed, put his hunting gun aside, took the flashlight out of his pocket and placed it next to the gun. He laid down on the bed and kept his eyes wide open so that he could get used to the darkness of the room as soon as possible and be ready for any appropriate reaction. He even stuck one of his hands to the gun so that he could have it and use it without wasting time if necessary. The sound of the rain, which had now intensified, and the roar of lightning made him more restless. For a moment, he gathered all his courage and closed his eyes. But he could not forget the moment of throwing the Holy Orb into the fire. It is as if he can hear the sound of the orb hitting the fireplace now, and with it, first silence and then the noise of those sitting in the café reacted to this behaviour. Even in that commotion, he heard the voice of one of them, who shouted angrily, "You will see the result of your deeds tonight." And the other said, "The Holy Orb knows how to defend itself well, so that no one will dare to do or insult it, even in private." Two people even rushed to him to teach him a lesson where they were stopped by the intervention of others and how bravely he stood in front of them. These situations were not in line with his current situation and acted as an alarm bell for him, announcing to him that his disrespect would not go unanswered. In fact, it was the first time he had acted so extremist. At that moment, he saw himself as a hero standing in front of rotten human structures and trying to save them. By doing so, he wanted to prove to everyone that people are captivated by wrong ideas and continue to make mistakes. But now that he was thinking well, he did not choose the right path, and it was better to act more confidently. Because he considered himself a civilised person, but his behaviour yesterday was not in his dignity. He believed that the people had deluded themselves and sanctified the golden orb and placed it everywhere.

A voice came from downstairs. Suddenly, he opened his eyes and involuntarily took the gun in his hand and sat up. He picked up the flashlight. He remained motionless to make sure he heard a sound. After a while, he heard the sound again. The sound of footsteps of a person or people walking on the wooden floor of a building and being careful that no one heard it. He did the same. He got up and slowly put his foot on the wooden floor. Because he was not sure how many people were waiting for him, and because he was upstairs and did not want them to notice him, he did not turn on the light and slowly went to the door of the room and opened it and looked out with one eye. The dim light from the lampshade on the ground floor allowed him to dominate the living room a bit and to be able to monitor the situation. But his view in the bedroom was limited, and he had to leave the room. He waited a while. He felt the shadow dance inside the light of the lampshade and the fireplace. Although he was not sure, he could not be indifferent. Slowly, he prepared his gun, turned on his flashlight, opened the bedroom door and went out towards the stairs as he held himself against the wall. He had to be careful. Now he could easily monitor the room. He saw shadows that were completely moving without making a sound. There were more than he could have imagined. Fear had taken over his whole being. He did not know what to do. He even thought it would be better to go back into the room and lock the door behind him. Maybe they came to steal his valuables. In any case, he was in good financial condition and everyone knew that he was living alone. So it was a good reason for them to be present, and it had nothing to do with what happened in the cafe yesterday. But another voice came from the adjoining room, questioning all his hypotheses. Suddenly, he turned, and the end of his shotgun hit an ornamental vase on the side of the stairs and fell, making a terrible noise. The voice echoed in the silence of the building, and he shouted involuntarily, "Who is there?" And he slowly approached the bedroom and asked again in the same decisive voice, "Who is there?" But h e did not hear again. He turned on the flashlight and went to the hallway in front of him. He did not dare to open the door of the room. He checked all the angles of the door with his flashlight and with great care, as he aimed his gun, turned the doorknob and pushed the door open with his fingertips and raised the flashlight. He entered the room slowly and was on the doorstep. The gun in one hand and the flashlight in the other did not give him a chance to turn on the light. On the other hand, suddenly the light of the flashlight fell on someone's face. He recognised him. He was the man who had warned him the day before who said he would see the results of his actions. His face was red and his eyes twinkled in the light of the flashlight, as if ready to attack him. He fired involuntarily, quickly preparing the gun again and pointing the flashlight in the other direction. He checked everywhere. But no one was there anymore. He wanted to go to the key and turn on the light, when suddenly the flashlight showed strange creatures in front of him. He saw they tried to attack him with a scary mood and Holy Orbs in their hands. He could not even recognise what creatures they were. He also shot at them and immediately lost his flashlight and fell down. In the same darkness and haste, he reloaded his gun and fired a third and fourth time. He reached for the door and turned on the key. It lit up everywhere. But no one was there. Everything was quiet. He picked up the flashlight from the floor. Now the sound of footsteps could be heard from his bedroom. He did not know what to do. At the same time, he heard other sounds indicating that they were coming up the stairs. He turned and panicked and went to his bedroom and without opening the door started firing and pierced the door and returned immediately. With trembling hands, he reloaded his gun, this time firing at the stairs until he realised he no longer had a cartridge. His gaze fell on the shadows, which showed strange creatures, and he shouted loudly, "What do you want from me? I did not want to throw the orb in the fire." Suddenly, as he was stepping back, his back hit something; he screamed in horror and felt that someone had grabbed him by the throat. Red light flooded the entire building. The gun fell from his hand, and he grabbed his throat with the fingers of both hands to try to free himself. He felt that he could no longer breathe and was suffocating. On the other hand, he saw creatures approaching him. He staggered to the hallway so that at the first opportunity he could release himself and go down the stairs and reach the exit and ask for help. But the suffocation on one side and the broken bites of the pot under his feet caused him to lose his balance and suddenly fall down the stairs with his head.

After a few days of absence, people waited in front of his building for the police to open the building. The torrential rains for several days meant that no one heard the sound of gunfire and no one understood his absence. But now that the weather was sunny, his absence was fully felt. After the door of the building was opened, he was seen lying motionless on the first stairs and dying of blood loss. As they lifted him, they noticed a bruise on his neck with fingerprints. They also found his gun in front of the bedroom. Police said the cause of his death was the presence of thieves that rainy night and that they would be looking for them.

Pranic

Pranic[*]

He hurried to the main hall. Cold sweat ran down his face and he tried to control the situation with short breaths. Fear had taken over his whole being and he did not really know what had happened. He stood and looked at his hands. He turned them a little. He was delusional. He thought blood was flowing from them, but they seemed perfectly normal. The only thing that was strange was the trembling of his hands, which was clearly visible even under the light of the candles that lit the hall. He opened and closed the fingers of both hands several times to show that there was no problem. But the sound of his heartbeat was so loud that it made him

---

Pranic Healing is an energy therapy system popularised by Chua Kok Soo. He believes that prana or life energy can be used to cleanse and cure diseases. He says Pranic therapy is similar to acupuncture and yoga, which can heal the body through the body's energy. Prana is a Sanskrit word meaning life energy. The presence of this energy causes health and life. In Eastern culture, it is known as CHI and KI.

lose focus. Undoubtedly, the space he was in added to his deteriorating mood. A large hall with tall columns and velvet curtains that did not allow any light to exchange between inside and outside. A few valuable paintings also hung on the walls of the hall, and a few candles barely lit up the interior. Some simple but valuable furniture was also part of the hall. He knew that the night before, but the worry and anxiety, along with the fear that had taken hold of him, prevented him from concentrating and rescuing himself from the predicament in which he had fallen. Now he was looking at himself as a therapist, desperately looking for a way out of a situation that had virtually no end but destruction. His eyes shook with the help of his hands, making matters worse than he thought. He did not think that he had lost the ability to control energies and internal and external forces. Perhaps it was because of the hands that had now become a demonic tool instead of a cure, and pollution had spread throughout it. Absolute silence had become the background music of the hall, which intensified his mood. It was as if he was sitting in his office just yesterday, treating his clients.

After a hard day, he was drinking a cup of coffee and began to send energy to have fun. At first, he thought that it would be better to replace the drink in his hand with a cup of hot coffee but not by calling the secretary but only by sending energy, to inspire the secretary to open the room and hold another cup in his hand. It seemed simple and rudimentary, because he was doing much harder work during the day. Just when one of his clients asked him to be healed and he masterfully treated him with his own specific healing methods that were rooted in some kind of energy healing. He then thought that he might need to call a friend for more fun, but as he thought about it and persuaded him, his cell phone rang. But he did not answer. Because he just wanted to present a show of his imaginative power in order to get rid of the tiredness of the day by believing in it and how powerful he is. Maybe he had some kind of daily life or maybe because he spent days and nights alone and tired of the routine of those around him, he needed to remind himself that he was a healer. A person who knows his job well and is somewhat aware of the affairs of the universe and knows when and where he can control the situation by giving special energies through his powerful hands. He sometimes thought that he was an exceptional person who could go beyond what was destined for man and that this was what had already isolated him and made him a tool for healing problems. They were used physically and mentally. He was dissatisfied with being limited and using the great potential he had for such purposes, and he felt that he had lost this great talent and had to do something with it that was beyond the ordinary routine. A kind of ambition pervaded his whole being, convincing him to address the universe this time with the talent he possessed in order to make a fundamental change in his present situation, which was full of daily repetitions. But he knew he had to focus more this time around because he wanted more than just a simple treatment or a cup of hot coffee or a phone call. He wanted something to happen that would save him from this state of lethargy. So he took a deep breath and found himself in a special situation and in front of a great position. He tried to add more detail to it with his visual power. At first, he imagined that it was located in a magnificent space and in a beautiful palace where a lot of wealth was accumulated. Then he thought of the kinds of food and drink that were there and how its owner could easily live there without a moment's work and out of laziness and how he could, with the utmost desire, take advantage of the power of his wealth to use and be proud to have it and how easily he can satisfy the desire for lust in himself. He was a little jealous of such a situation and was angry with himself for not thinking about it all these years and how he has been taking care of people's affairs like a simple therapist all this time.

He was looking for a way out. He looked around. In the corner of the hall, there was a staircase that moved in a semicircle to the upper floor. Maybe from there he could get into space and get rid of the terrible magic of that night. He reached for the stairs and looked desperately at the dark end before climbing it. Maybe it would be better to find another way to get out of there. But excitement and anxiety overwhelmed him so much that his decision-making power was completely disrupted, and he thought only of one thing: how he could get out of the palace hall in the shortest possible time and save himself. It was utterly impossible for him to imagine what he had done with both hands out of tolerance and digestion. For the last time, with an illusion in his eyes, he spun around the hall quickly so that he might find a way out. He was sure he could not turn back the way he had come. He reached the stairs again. He had to leave before others knew he was in the hall. Now, if this was the way out, it would be through a staircase that ended in complete silence and darkness. He stood up again and looked at his hands. He felt blood gushing from them like a boiling spring. He took them firmly to his face and placed them over his eyes and involuntarily began to cry. All his emotions were intertwined, and he involuntarily heard the laughter of a man whose hands no longer seemed insignificant to him. He put his foot on the stairs and went up.

The stairs of the palace had a special glory. He was able to persuade the king of the palace to send a messenger to invite him to the palace and solve the king's problem. A voice came into his room and he had involuntarily allowed him to enter. The king's messenger entered and looked at him curiously. Then he took a letter out of his bag and gave it to him and at the same time explained that the king had not been in a good mood for some time and was constantly spending his time in nightmares and fears, and since the therapist's fame was all over, today they concluded that he might be able to find a solution to this issue, which would certainly be praised by the king. He looked at the messenger and at the same time took the letter from him and opened it and looked at it. Undoubtedly, this was the same energetic feedback that he had thought about a few moments before, and the image that was etched in his mind could be related to the palace that he must now step into and see in reality. Surely, this invitation could have been a turning point for him, transforming him from a simple healer into a person who is praised by the great people and freed from the kind of monotony that had taken over his whole life. He knew how to use prana, which is a life force and greet the king with this invisible life-giving energy.

He passed through the waiting room and entered the bedroom. A room full of splendour and with a special beauty in which a huge fortune was gathered. In disbelief, he saw a king lying on a throne in front of him, with beautiful crews guarding him. He placed a variety of drinks and snacks in front of the bed, and he, too, looked at them with disgust and lethargy and did not want them. His high weight indicated that he was not motivated or rather unwilling to continue. The therapist stared at him and immediately, as he had told the king's messenger before treatment, all the crew left.

The therapist and the king were now alone in a large room overlooking the hall. He looked at the king. Then he pointed to his surroundings and talked about his unfavourable situation. The therapist, who felt that he was acting cautiously among the many issues and facts, smiled and interrupted him, asking him to refrain from hiding the issues and facts in front of him and to tell him exactly what things upset him and put him in such a situation, and then he insisted that he refrain from any concealment and consider him as a therapist and physician, so that he, too, with sufficient information, could make decisions and use the energy of life and act correctly and in a timely manner. The king, who found himself in the shelter of the energising forces, and because he was utterly offended by his present condition, gently looked at the therapist and confessed all that had been declared to be great sins. Even in his confessions, he declared that this was simply because of the situation in which he found himself and that he did not like to commit such sins at all and now he finds himself in a position that brings him nothing but annoyance and remorse. And anxiety, along with fear and delusion of what he has done, has overwhelmed him.

As the sentences flowed explicitly by the king, each moment evoked a new feeling for the therapist. He sometimes envied and was jealous, and sometimes he became so angry that he could not control himself. When he saw the king in a situation where power, glory and wealth had turned him into a creature from which pride arose and caused his unhappiness and distress, he felt jealousy and anger and a kind of longing that he wished could be like him. But he tried to be rational and not forget his therapeutic position, which is associated with healing energies. He stared at him and tried not to speak during his confession. He was silent until the king, whose face was covered in cold sweat, and his eyes, from which the illusion was rippling, were silenced. He could easily hear the sound of the king's heartbeat. Tears welled up in his eyes, and a look of anxiety and worry about the future, which no longer existed for him, appeared on his face. This was the first time that the therapist enjoyed seeing such a scene and found himself on the verge of demonic forces. He enjoys the fact that a person in such a position has been harassing others for a long time and now, desperate for his sins, has involuntarily suffered some kind of fear and nervous breakdown. He could not believe how the king had been able to influence him and bring him to the level of a demonic force that had changed from a healer to a destructive person, as if prana no longer existed in the universe and all that is existed is demonic forces that has come to the help of man.

He climbed the stairs one by one. He had exactly the same feeling that the ruler had suffered a few minutes before. The stairs seemed so large that he could not see the power to reach the end. He was sure that the way out of the demonic forces was only possible by climbing the stairs and there was no other way. Gradually, he became more determined as he went through each of the steps, knowing that he had chosen the right path this time. To maintain his balance, he leaned on the railing, helped to climb it and placed his weight on the railing. It seemed that everything was coming to an end and soon he could escape from inside the palace. He could no longer feel the trembling of his hands, but this time, it was his legs that could not bear his weight. He moved up a few steps. He stood for a moment and looked behind him. The hall was plunged into darkness and silence. There seemed to be no time to go back, especially when he heard the voices of the king's officers and bodyguards who were looking for him. He did not seem to have enough time in his office to get a clear idea of what he wanted.

Perhaps it would be better to think about the future and some changes when the conditions were right, to create a clearer picture with more details and then to send the necessary energy. Only a few moments had passed from the time the energy was sent to the time of its execution and the arrival of the king's messenger in his office, which meant the ruin of his life and all the power that had made him special to others. He climbed another step, this time knowing exactly what had happened. He no longer blamed himself, and this time instead of prana, he used demonic forces to heal his patient, transforming him from a healer to a complete destroyer. But now, he was satisfied, because he saw himself and the king doomed to seven sins, both of which they had equally suffered, and such people are doomed to the same fate.

He went to the king. He looked at him and asked him to take a few deep breaths, to visualise a white orb and to think of nothing but what the therapist was saying so that he could inject prana energy into his body and contaminate him with any clean and pure things. The therapist then came to the king and examined him from head to toe with his hands, without his hands touching his body. As he moved his hands a few inches around him, he reconsidered everything he had said. At first, he thought he could get the negative energies out of his patient's mind. But he later thought that saving him would be a betrayal of all those who had been harmed by the king during this time. When the king spoke proudly of his fame and power, eagerly pursuing and pointing to his aspirations, anger pervaded the healer's whole being, and he found himself in the position of one who could do justice. Suddenly, demonic forces overpowered him, and he saw his hands on the king's throat, and instead of holding his head to expel the negative energies, he squeezed his neck with all his might, seeing him as the cause of all the darkness of the earth. The king, too, seemed pleased with his fate and did not resist in order to escape his terrifying anxiety and nervousness, until the healer rushed out of his room with his hands dirty with the king's sins, which he had now laid quietly on the bed. He came out and reached the hall, as if he had intended the best treatment for him. And now, through the transfer of energy, all the negative energies were transferred to his therapist, who drove him crazy and insane to the stairs to save himself from the king's officers and bodyguards.

At the same time, disturbed and worried, and with the sound of the guards, which made him most nervous, he took the last few steps and reached the upper floor. He thought for a moment that he wished he had not imagined that in his office yesterday, but he soon thought he was a healer, and this time, instead of fighting the negative energies of his clients, he went to war with demonic forces and again as a healer, he has cleared the earth from pollution. Then he reached the balcony, the height was perfect, and at the same time, he looked at his hands in which the pollution was rippling, and before the guards reached him and their hands became dirty the same as him, he surrendered to another world.

Lotus

Lotus[*]

The sound of shouting filled all the streets of the city, and nothing but the sound of destruction and terror could be heard. Men and women rushed everywhere, and sometimes children were left in the middle of the way. The dust had

---

[*]**Lotus** *or the Egyptian lotus is the national flower of Egypt. This flower is also one of the national symbols of Iran and can be seen in the lithographs of Parseh (Persepolis). A species of this flower called the Holy Lotus is the symbol of the city of Kermanshah and the colour of that flower is the symbolic colour of this city. The name of this flower in Persian is Pahlavi Niloofar, which means a flower with indigo feathers. The lotus flower is a plant that grows in deep ponds and river water that does not flow fast and its leaves are very wide and green in the shape of a heart that is placed on the surface of the water and with a petiole that is the size of a finger, attached to the root. The lotus flower opens in the morning and closes at night, using a root-like underground stem to attach itself to a sludge or sandy ground. This plant has medicinal benefits, but it has a narcotic property that overuse can cause forgetfulness.*

darkened the sky, and at every moment, a terrible sound added to the turmoil. Everyone was looking for a shelter to hide in this chaos. But the catastrophe was beyond survival. No one knew anyone else, and they passed each other carelessly. In a corner of the city, a great fire was kindled, the flames of which ruthlessly engulfed everything. The people of the city had given up the resistance and were wandering aimlessly, and on their way, they sometimes set foot on bodies that were alive several hours ago. Every sound that arose made some people fall to the ground, and they, too, remained motionless, staring at infinity with fixed, open eyes, as if they had been so from the beginning. On the other hand, there was a voice in the crowd calling for calm. But that voice was not loud enough to convince people, and it was soon forgotten amid the commotion.

The phone rang repeatedly in the adjoining rooms, and the leader was sitting in his rocking chair alone in his office, staring into the distance, as if nothing had happened. Perhaps he was accustomed to the awkward noises outside of his office and considered them part of his afternoon. He had experienced worse in his life and did not understand the reason for this panic. Maybe people are scared and have lost their discernment. He could not believe how the people of the city had simply lost faith in him and his thoughts. He had always devoted himself to them, so they should have paid more attention in these unfavourable circumstances and resisted for the survival of the leader. Maybe they had forgotten their past. It was he who was able to introduce them to the new utopia. They themselves were aware of this. In a day when all of them had no hope for tomorrow, it was the guide who paved the way for them with great self-sacrifice and did not allow them to fall into the hands of people who knew nothing of humanity. All this time, he was thinking of their happiness and seeking their way of salvation, and now that he was imprisoned in his office, he expected them to sacrifice for him. Now his office phone rang. Although he had ordered that no telephone be connected, it was as if even his clerk no longer obeyed his orders. He could no longer trust anyone. The evidence showed this. Over the past few weeks, he has heard over and over again that people have lost faith in the leader, and even a group has thought of killing him. Sometimes he thought that maybe in some cases he was a little extremist, and maybe it was better to look at things more calmly. But he soon convinced himself that the leader was in everyone's best interest and that this was exactly what the leader had been suffering from lately, and he never wanted such an issue to even cross his mind. He still considered himself the only supporter of the city and used his decisions for the betterment of the city. He did not even like for a moment to think that this was the cause of all his chaos. While he considered himself the defender of the city, he had repeatedly stated in his sermons that the way of salvation was what the leader led them to, because he was the one who had enlightened the sense of power among the people, and now he was the victim. He liked to have the opportunity to tell people for the last time that the truth was what he had mentioned many times in his speeches. But did saying that change anything? There was a sense of confusion and depression in his eyes. He waited for the bell of clock to ring five times and for the maid to arrive with his favourite drink. He was the one who always paid special attention to order and all his employees and even all the people of the city knew about it. He had emphasised this many times, and it was always said that the leader has a special skill in guiding people. It was even the people who called him their leader and saw him as their saviour. He became the hero of the people who promised them the golden age of the coming days and asked all of them to participate in this path. Apparently, it was only yesterday that he was standing on the balcony of his office, saying things that everyone was excited about and all of them were calling his name. He was no longer just a leader but a hero that the people of the city had been looking for and waiting for years and had given him a holy face. Some praised him and carried out his orders without any thought. Because he was the leader who knew everything and knew how to guide them.

The alarm went off, and he turned his gaze to the door after a long time, but no one entered. That could not be true. He should drink his favourite drink on time so that he can think better about people's problems. It was an unforgivable sin he could never forgive. The sound of unanswered telephones in the adjoining rooms was still everywhere. Finally, the leader got up and went to the balcony. A kind of fear had taken over his whole being. He did not want to remove the curtain. He thought there were scenes on the other side of the screen that could hurt his pride. He had many plans for the development of the city. But he was only a little unlucky and his calculations were messed up. There was still a chance to get everything back to normal. People should have understood him a little. He never wanted to witness moments he had not even thought about. His arms and legs were shaking. He gently pulled back the curtain and then opened the door. Abnormal noises rushed into the room. He went a little further. He could not step into a place that last had a large population in front of him and was now being replaced by ruins. He smelled smoke and fire. At the bottom of the building, on the other side of the courtyard, he could see that the guard posts were on fire. He did not see in himself the power to stand there anymore and witness the destruction of the city. Weakness had taken over his whole being. He could not even return to the room. He leaned his hand against the wall and came in slowly, trying to close the door. He thought to himself that he was a true leader and could bring everything back to normal. Everyone still loves and serves him. At the same time, the door opened and his special clerk rushed in without knocking, and he saw him in the corner of the room and came to him and immediately handed him the folded piece of paper on which an important message was written, and without waiting, he left the room quickly. The leader's hands were so shaky that he could not open the note, and as he tried to keep his balance, he leaned against the wall and reached for his desk to take care of things. This was the room where the elders of the city gathered to hear his instructions, and he advised them from behind his desk with strength and firmness. He reached behind the table and sat down on his chair. He thought that nothing had happened and then pressed the alarm button to let the maid into the room. But no one entered. If he did not hear or did not know the servant's bell, he would have thought that the bell might be broken. But after a while, he thought that perhaps the servant had not heard the bell amidst all the hustle and bustle. So he picked up the phone and dialled the clerk. No one answered. It was possible that conflicts outside the office caused everyone to be busy. He put the phone back in place. It was as if he was trying to pass the time and read the message in his hand later. He opened it with the same trembling hands and repeated the sentences under his lips. After reading each sentence, his frown became more and more confused, as if his real self, like one of the employees outside the office, was running away. He dropped the paper, got up from his desk and walked over to the conference table, which had a map on it that marked his office among all the different cities. He saw his employees circling around him, praising him. But it had been a while since he had not talked about future plans and this had discouraged him. Desperate, he turned to the window that led to the backyard. He opened the window and looked out. In front of him were lotus flowers on a small garden lake. He stared at them. A beautiful image that affected the calmness of the leader in critical situations and saved him for a moment from every thought he had in his head. Looking at the flowers of the sacred lotus had calmed his mental crises, and he found himself away from the hustle and bustle. It seemed that it might be better for him to live for himself, because these people did not deserve his presence and did not understand the reality of his existence. He never wanted so much destruction, but there were no conditions that could be easily consulted to achieve the desired result. He considered himself the leader of all and had no doubt in this matter and he obliged the people to follow him. It was a unique sight. He just wished he had looked at the lotus flowers that were still open a few hours ago. They needed to rest, and their leaves hid the beautiful lotus flower, and their petals were closed. He turned inwards and made his way to the back door that led to the courtyard, and very soon, he found himself by the lake and involuntarily heard his voice speaking with all his might to the lotus. He kept in his heart everything he had been through all this time of turmoil, and he saw time as the best opportunity to express what he had not said. He then recalled the legend of Homer, in which Odysseus and his companions entered the island and lost their memory by eating the lotus fruit. Tears welled up in his eyes as he tried to stop the flow. He had not eaten for a long time. He went to the water and sat there. Then he picked up the lotus and looked at it. He no longer wanted to think about his failures. He did not even want to remember that he was a leader to the people. Then, with more trembling hands than before, he picked the lotus fruit and slowly and fearfully took it to his mouth, and very quickly and in a greater hurry, he took a few more into his mouth and ate them restlessly. After a short time, he looked at his hands. They did not tremble anymore. He turned and looked at the building behind him, everything seemed to be in order. He did not even hear a sound anymore. He raised his head. He saw a balcony in the centre of the building. He said to himself that he wished he could one day go to that room and see the holy lotus from there. Then he went back to the lake and did not remember how long he had been there. He walked along the shore of the lake and, whispering a poem under his lips, continued on his way and walked away.

The Queen of Loneliness

14

The Queen of Loneliness

When the queen arrived, all twelve members of the meeting stood up and waited for her to sit in her special seat. They looked at each other meaningfully and anxiously examined the queen's behaviour from under their eyes. Silence was everywhere, and no one allowed himself to speak in front of her. Conditions were not favourable, and this time, the castle was under siege, a kind of despair and disappointment overcame the people. Little by little, there was a rumour among the inhabitants of the castle that perhaps the queen should have made a better decision and not allow the situation to become so extreme that it would cause a lot of damage. But the queen was more determined than ever and acted in the best manner of her life. During these few months, many people intervened and even mediated, but every time one of them tried to end this issue, he faced the queen's anger and had a bad end for himself and his family. Even recently, her senior adviser, along with his physician, had complained about his recent behaviour and decisions, which resulted in their expulsion from the castle and their betrayal. Some people, seeing these cases, came to believe that the queen may have lost her temper and not make a wise decision, because when a special doctor takes her extremism, it must be a sign that she is no longer as usual and takes the castle to the brink of destruction with its inhabitants. But she believed that resisting the forces of evil was the only goal she pursued, and she never expected a pleasant news to reach her and her inhabitants from outside the castle walls. She was so decisive that she left no room for controversy, but during the longer siege, she created a kind of audacity among senior advisers to sometimes criticise her behaviour in her absence.

With a wave of her hand, she allowed the others to sit on their chairs, and they waited for her orders. Six people were sitting on one side of the table and six on the other, staring into each other's eyes, trying to pretend that the castle was in complete control and nothing to worry about. Then the queen, trying to portray a kind of holiness, smiled briefly and opened her mouth:

> "As you know, we are in a situation that is very important and sensitive, and you know that this waiting inside the castle and the resistance is very valuable, and of course, it is commendable. I am sure that with wisdom and carrying out the orders that are issued, we can manage this crisis and eliminate all the enemies that are waiting for us behind the walls. You know that the queen thinks only of the inhabitants of the castle and uses all her power to make them happy. Undoubtedly, the people who ostensibly called themselves friends

during this period, their truth has been revealed and gone, and now all those in front of me are among those forces who adhere to the queen's principles and want nothing but their own happiness and that of their families. As the queen and the first person of the castle, I assure them that victory will be for those who have faith and have no moment of doubt. Know that all those who once considered themselves friends and supporters of this castle, have now gathered outside it and blocked the way for its inhabitants, and this is not something that the queen will pass through. Do not pay attention to their cries and do not allow division among the inhabitants of the castle. If we are in such a situation right now, the first and last reason is for ourselves. We know the good of the castle and its inhabitants. How can some people claim that they are more worried about the castle and its people than we are? During this time, many people came and announced that the way to save the people of the castle is to get out of it and communicate with the people elsewhere. But it is quite obvious that if the queen is known and entitled as the Queen of Loneliness among them, it is because she knows very well that outside and behind the high walls of the castle, nothing but lies and deception await anyone. They think they can seduce the inhabitants and persuade them to surrender to the castle where they live. However, they deceived a few of my best people. But soon the end of their work will be seen in front of your eyes. Know that the queen thinks of nothing but the salvation of her people and never wants and will not let go of the comfort that the people of the castle enjoy today. It has been a long time and a lot of energy spent for these loyal residents and you, the senior advisers and commanders, to be able to live proudly among your family members, and today is the day that the queen intends to enter a new phase of resistance against their siege. I hope you are all ready to advance each and every one of the orders issued. Because no excuse is accepted in this regard and there is no forgiveness for those who do not fulfil their duties. You are fully aware of this issue. The inhabitants of the castle will no longer accept any reason for negligence or incompetence among you, the commanders and senior advisers."

She looked at them. They listened to the queen in complete astonishment and silence, and not a moment moved, and they did not take their eyes off the queen, and they looked as if they themselves had already guessed all the queen's behaviour and were fully prepared to obey all her orders. In order to give them one last warning, the queen turned her head towards them and looked deeply into their eyes that were staring at her, asking for their approval. It didn't matter to her, though, and she was just used to giving orders. But acknowledging her behaviour at a time when many of her friends were criticising her was something she sought and calmed her heart. Moments passed like this, then she turned to her servant, who was standing next to her, ready to serve, and said that she was waiting to hear the new news and that, before issuing a new order, which dealt with all the affairs of the castle, she asked to be aware of the outside of the castle and the besiegers so that no mistake can be made in guiding the inhabitants of the castle. However, he felt completely responsible for everything and never wanted the future of the castle to be jeopardised, especially when her closest relatives criticised her for her recent policies and she was forced to remove her senior adviser and special physician from the castle. At the same time, the secretary read from the papers in his hand while reading the statistics which showed that all the conditions were under control, constantly pointing out that the queen had predicted everything and was aware of everything, and with these sentences in this way, he instilled in other commanders and advisers that everything was planned in advance and that everything seemed to be going according to the queen's opinion. Every time this sentence came out of the secretary's mouth, the queen shook her head a little as a sign of appreciation and smiled so that others would be encouraged to know that all matters are under the strict supervision of the queen and in fact this is the only way of salvation. If they acknowledge this, they will pay special attention to the queen. Then the secretary lowered the papers and walked a little behind the queen and bowed. The queen also raised her left hand slightly to exempt him of his responsibilities. Then, with the same initial smile she had begun to speak, she looked at all twelve people and continued:

"You see, the queen oversees everything and even controls all the conditions but also manages them. Now that you understand what is happening outside the walls of the castle, you should also know that if we are sitting in the castle today alone, we are not captives at all, but we declare that we are far away from the society which affects the health of the inhabitants of the castle, and it is one of the duties of all people to defend, especially you dear ones. Many people want to liken this silence to captivity and take us away from the goal we are pursuing. This goal is what has made me the Queen of Loneliness among them, regardless of the fact that they are the ones who are lonely and spend their time in their ignorance. I am very happy that I have been able to keep my people in solitude and away from the hustle and bustle outside the castle and not allow myself and the people of the castle to be subjected to the abnormal behaviours that have arisen from their communities over the years. But today, if you are gathered here, it is not just information about these issues. Rather, I want to officially and without any excuse order you to fight and break this siege that has lasted for almost three months and call for a confrontation. Since all the forces are on standby during this time, I tell you that tomorrow morning, at dawn, we will attack the besiegers with the first shot and give a good lesson to all those who think they know everything, and others may not be able to analyse the situation. Tomorrow morning, we will attack them according to the plan that is in the hands of the secretary. After I leave, the secretary will provide you with this delicately designed map. I just emphasise that everything should go according to plan and none of you should ever be emotional in this regard and sometimes be gentle with those who call themselves friends, because the softness in this regard has cost them their lives. Of course, I think it is a heavy price, and I think that you, dear commanders and advisers, are wiser than to try to act contrary to what has been recommended to you, and to remind you of the seriousness and importance of the instructions, I ask my secretary to inform your friends."

He then glanced at the secretary, who hurried to the exit, pointing to those standing outside the hall. It was as if they are waiting for him. Soon the secretary, with a few men carrying the two boxes with difficulty, came to the queen again and very slowly said a few words in the queen's ear, and after the queen's approval, she simply shook her head slowly and with dignity. She pointed to those carrying the boxes to put them on the ground and to stay away from them. A red mark of blood stain could be seen all the way through both boxes. This was the first time during this period that the commanders and advisers were convinced that the queen had completely changed and that her decisions not only isolated her but also had a kind of violence in her behaviour. They could well have witnessed this violence, without even knowing exactly what awaited them inside the boxes. Watching their fear and paleness, the queen seemed satisfied and had achieved exactly what she wanted. The secretary then went to both boxes to open them and warn the castle's advisers and commanders, persuading them of what an uncertain future awaited them if they did not follow the orders. They no longer knew that there was no other way but to fight and that they were going to go to war early in the morning with people, some of whom had even entered the siege of the castle because of kindness and help the others.

Suddenly, he went up to the first box, and at that moment, an eerie voice rose from among the members of the meeting, some of whom subconsciously put their hands forward and covered their faces and some of them turned their heads to never see more of the scene in front of them. There was something in front of them and inside the box that they had never imagined. The lifeless and blood-soaked body of the senior adviser was inside, with his right hand protruding from the box, which could be clearly identified from the tattoo written on his hand without looking at his face, which showed itself with a special line under the bloodstains. "We are loyal to the queen," he wrote. And perhaps this was exactly the reward the queen had given him, as if it were the queen who was not loyal to herself. At the same time, the secretary opened the second box, so it was no longer difficult to guess what was in the second box. It was quite clear that in the second box there could be no one but a special physician, because the queen's physician had done much worse than the senior adviser. It was by protesting that the queen was no longer the former queen and had lost her decision-making power. They all guessed right. The lifeless face of the special physician was displayed on the box. Then the queen, who seemed to be quite successful from this performance, suddenly stood up and shouted, "Long live the Queen of Loneliness!" Meanwhile, all the commanders and advisers saw themselves involuntarily acting like the queen and shouting in one voice,

"Long live the Queen of Loneliness!" These words were repeated for a few minutes until their unity came to the eyes of the queen. The queen then invited them to be silent and raised her hand in the sense that she wanted to continue her speech. After a moment of silence, the queen continued:

> "Tomorrow is a day of destiny, and we prove to everyone that if we had been silent and stayed inside the castle, it was not because we were afraid or weak but because we thought we might be giving others a chance to tell them that it is better to think. T h e queen and the castle are not afraid of them but because she does not want to harm them, and in her opinion, all these people are sinners who want to pollute the peace in the castle, with the same sins that they committed themselves during the times. Different people commit it, and if we avoid them, it is simply because we know our worth."

The queen then pointed to the secretary, and he, too, ordered a few drinks be brought to the queen and others. Then the queen drank to congratulate her victory and this great decision. The queen continued after drinking a sip of it:

> "The victory is ours and tomorrow I will officially declare that war is beginning, with the first arrow coming out of the bow."

Then she got up, looked at the members around the conference table and headed for the exit. Concern is rippling through the eyes of all members. It was as if they were waiting for something big to happen, and what brought them together was not the news of a declaration of war. They did not seem to be terrified of hearing the order of war and may have come to believe that the senior adviser and special physician were completely innocent, and that they themselves might be the next victims. No one moved, and all eyes were on the exit, watching the queen walk away. Meanwhile, the queen stood. The moment remained motionless. Then he turned and, anxiously never seen before, pointed to the drink with a trembling hand, and suddenly, before she could speak, put her hand to her throat, and so that she could no longer speak, she became motionless. She fell to the ground. The secretary and two of the servants hurried towards her anxiously trying to find out the cause and rush to the queen's aid. Meanwhile, one of the advisors turned to the others and said:

> "The Queen of Loneliness reached the peace she had spoken and promised. Tomorrow, as decided, we will open the castle door and end the siege."

Hourglass

Hourglass[*]

"It was my turn."

He said this and hurried out of the building. The fog was everywhere. He could feel the moisture on his cheeks. With each passing moment, he became more and more frightened and tried his best not to lose his focus. The fear of the end was so great that he felt a kind of weakness and lethargy in his whole being, but he tried not to pay attention to it because it could keep him from continuing. The streets were completely dark and the lights barely lit the way. There was no one on the streets, and it was clear that everything was pre-planned and that special moment had been set aside for

---

__Hourglass:__ is a type of chronometer invented by a priest in the eighth century. The hourglass consists of two glass bubbles glued together with a narrow hole for sand to pass through, so that the sand gradually moves from the top bubble to the bottom bubble. The container was then turned upside down and the same operation was repeated. As the number of times the sand moved through the bubbles became known, the approximate time was determined.

him to cross, so that he could pass the final stage alone. Perhaps he never imagined that his turn would come, or that he would experience a time when in full consciousness, he would be informed of his turn. At first, he thought he might be deluded and there was still enough time for it. But he could feel with all his being that he was like a stranger who did not even see the power to stay. He even thought for a moment that perhaps the most important thing was to get through this stage, and that if he was told that they had made a mistake, it would still have no effect on the whole affair, and now that he had fully tasted the panic, it would be better to complete the work and pass through the streets and the people who have become strangers to him now. There was a kind of depression on his face with the horror of walking. He tried to control himself, but the anxiety that he would not reach his destination on time made him anxious. He increased his speed and started running, thinking that he should do his best. A strange silence was everywhere, and his only hope was the path in his mind. The streets were all the same, making it difficult for him to find his way. He had been wandering in them for a while, and every time he went to the street, he felt that he had been there for a while. Little by little, he came to believe that he would never get where he wanted to go. He was so scared that he did not even have the strength or courage to stop. With each passing moment, things got worse. The lights became dimmer and the streets darker. It was starting to rain, and strange noises were heard from the animals. Their howls promised his presence and they waited every moment for him to fall. These were exactly the symptoms he had been thinking about since he was a child. Rushing through the streets, he found himself on the threshold of narrower streets. The lights of the buildings were turned off one after the other, preparing the stage for his presence. From what he feared, the situation was decided for him. Still unstable, he was sure he was lost, and he was so sorry for the situation that he could not stop blaming himself at a time when it was even his turn. He had passed through these streets for years, thinking over and over again that it was better to go there before it was announced that it was his turn. But each time, there was a problem that caused him to put it off, and now that he saw himself as possible at the last moment, he could not find a way. He no longer saw the correct interpretation of fear. All he knew was that he felt a strong interest in what he wanted, and he wanted to get there no matter what awaited him. It was raining heavily and he was still wandering the streets. He saw shadows that sometimes chase after him and sometimes turn around him and even pass by him. At first, he did not pay attention to them, but their growing presence meant that the remaining opportunity was coming to an end. He glanced at himself as he ran. Undoubtedly, his current condition proved that he himself is in the form of the same shadows that join him every moment from the surrounding streets in his path. He could not even interpret time correctly; he only knew that the last grains of sand were crumbling from inside the hourglass. He stared again and again at the falling sand, but very soon, with a sudden turn, he would start all over again and forget everything. But this time, he saw himself as the sand falling and perhaps waiting to return to its original state by rotating. He firmly believed that the last grains would always fall faster, and he found himself on the verge of a fall that was accelerating at every moment, and without waiting any longer, and without any difference, it was his turn and he had to pass through the same places, that his predecessors have gone through. A lasting justice that he, too, had bowed down to without any reason and perhaps more easily than anyone else and more independent of all and had come out of the building at a faster speed than those present and had run to the street. He had not even had a chance to say goodbye to his friends and hug his loved ones, and he had cruelly locked the building behind him and had not remembered them even once since he had been on the streets. He continued on his way so carelessly that he did not even think about them, while lately he remembered every time his turn and how he left his loved ones, his whole face filled with tears. Maybe it wasn't him who was moving in that direction, and maybe a huge force was pushing him forward or moving him. But if so, why was he lost and could not find the main way? He was sure that his path of hope was in one of those streets that he had passed over and over again and forgotten. He looked at the shadows. It was as if they had the same problem he was dealing with. Although he did not recognise their faces, their confusion testified to this. He tried to follow in their footsteps. Maybe they, too, at the time of their turn were thinking of the place he was looking for. But they were so similar that it was impossible to distinguish them, and sometimes they went astray. On the other hand, the rain had intensified so much with the frequent thunderstorms that his eyes had lost the way, and all he could see was darkness, with the shadows disappearing one after the other before they reached their destination. But maybe he still had some moments left. He gathered the rest of his strength and started running again. Suddenly, he saw a flicker of light in front of him and ran towards it with double will. He could feel himself climbing the stairs there. He knew it was not closed there. He had passed through it many times at different times and was always open there, although few people were there, always waiting for passers-by alone. Maybe everyone, like him, had postponed their presence until it was their turn. So he had to face a lot of people.

In disbelief, he found himself in front of the church, where he stood in difficult conditions and took refuge in that torrential rain. Although he could no longer feel the cold, he reluctantly entered the building to protect himself from the bite of nature. Whatever it was, it was absolute calm that mocked him. The dancing light of lighted candles among the high walls gave him such warmth that even when he no longer felt anything, he still understood it. The wooden benches in front of him were so tidy that when the door of church closed and after he entered, it brought nothing but silence and calm. Its splendour was so dazzling that he forgot what hardships he had endured to enter its last moment. As he wondered what awaited him if he did not get here, he found himself crossing the corridor between the benches, which miraculously led him to the altar. In front of him, he saw sculptures hanging from the ceiling and walls, depicting the ability of their Creator with lasting elegance. The light of the candle flames also affected their beauty. Subconsciously, he looked at the candles and involuntary saw himself in front of them. He could not be a spectator anymore, so he reached out to them to light a candle and help the beauty there. He was sure that he would do his best, but he was not able to remove even one of the candles from the box and light it. He felt sadness in his being. But this was not the only time he had been there. He had been there many times in the past but did not feel the need to light any candles. So why did he grieve this time? And it was as he heard his voice answering him:

"Because it's my turn…"

This time, after saying this sentence, he did not feel any restlessness and was sure that he had accepted. He rejoiced at the reception and his last presence inside the churchyard, and while he was sure that this was the last thing he was experiencing, he listened to the musicians inside the church sing along with the choir, which sang:

"It was my turn."

Magic Box

Magic Box

This was for several consecutive nights that he had involuntarily turned into a sleepwalker in the jungle, who had come a long way, and during all this time, as if he had been transformed, he thought of nothing but walking. In fact, he was not at all sure whether he was asleep or consciously doing so. His behaviour seemed completely abnormal. Even the bravest members of the tribe did not have the courage to walk for hours in the dark, among the big trees and at the risk of predators, without any torches and without losing their way back, to reach the village at sunrise, and whenever he is asked why he risked his life, then he shows with a surprised look that he does not remember anything. But the wounds on his legs, which had passed through the thick grass and sometimes injured him, along with the mud of the rivers that had dried on his feet, showed that he was hiding something from everyone. Sometimes, when he returned to the village at night, the people of the tribe would ask themselves what he was looking for in the dark, but he was fainting in the cottage where he lived, with unsuitable conditions and pale colours. Certainly, the trembling of his hands and the fever of his forehead carried a message, but his silence showed that he was never inclined to explain and preferred not to be asked about it. Perhaps he should have left himself alone until news of his death by jungle animals or found his body among the rocks that stood firmly in the middle of the river. But that did not make sense. In any case, he was considered a relative of the chief of the tribe, and this was partly an insult to him. On the other hand, there was enough superstition, fear and panic among the members of the tribe who lived in the heart of the jungle, and if he was left alone and had a calamity, he would be asked for several generations what would happen to him. Was he cursed? So the most logical way was to follow him to find out the cause of his nightmares and sleepwalking. However, the opinion of a limited number of tribal elders was that he should be eliminated, because perhaps this behaviour of him will cause unpleasant events that will affect them as well. However, when he returned from the jungle, it was so unusual that even the decision of these people seemed logical. Some also believed that such sensitivities were unreasonable and that he might have lost his senses and his behaviours were not so important. But the question was, why did nothing happen to him every night he left the village? It certainly could not have been so long, and of course, behind-the-scenes teams were helping him. But he's taking advantage of the tribal chief's wealth and importance for his family situation, so why did he have to show behaviour that frightened or made everyone in the tribe suspicious?

So at the request of one of the village elders and without the knowledge of the chief of the tribe, a council was formed to decide on this matter. Any error could have irreparable effects. On the other hand, the chief of the tribe was popular enough among the villagers that his unhappiness could even threaten the existing order in the tribe. The seven-member council decided to follow up with him to answer their questions, and since no one should know about this, it was decided that the pursuers would be from the same council members, do not disrupt the tribal order until the desired result is achieved or even act cautiously and find out, without the tribal chief noticing. But this had many difficulties. Initially, people who were young and able to follow him as long as he continued to walk and sleep should be selected. On the other hand, they had to chase him without having a torch in his hand so that he would not be informed of their presence, and this was very difficult, because even the tribal elders who lived in the darkness of the forest for years could not carry out such a great danger without a lighted torch. They even considered that he might disturb them.

***

The death of the chief of the tribe, though sudden, left the successors free to prepare for any possible danger. Of course, this issue overshadowed his years of travel and he was forgotten for a while in the midst of tribal events. The new rulers of the tribe were about to enact laws that they had not had time to make in the decades before the previous chief, and he continued to wander around occasionally, as if the possibility of any danger had disappeared. He reached the top of a hill that was completely covered with wild plants and grass and surrounded by large trees. This was the first time he saw himself there. He waited for a while to examine the situation, but as always, a strange force called him. Although the path was in complete darkness, he felt that he saw everything and had the ability to find what he was looking for. The only problem was that he did not know what he was looking for and was going to continue to do so for a few more years. Of course, his presence on that hill for the first time may be a sufficient reason to end the situation that has preoccupied him during these years. He followed his legs, which were moving involuntarily, until he stood in front of a big tree. Where he stood, the moon, in full form, sent the lightest into the jungle, and he saw for the first time his eyes twinkle and search for something. He did not have a proper understanding of the suspicious sounds he heard. Although he was afraid to hear them, he felt that they might be showing the way. Time and place no longer meant anything to him. But he knew that everything was related to the tree in front of him. He slowly turned around and found a compartment in its trunk that had enough space to hide a large treasure. He put his hands inside the compartment and soon found a box in his hands. He took it out. A small box made of wood with special delicacy. At the same time, he heard voices that sounded like hymns, and this was the first time that he had his five senses at work again. He could smell the joy and the anthem that filled the air, and he could well feel that a group was dancing around him. Although no one was around, he could feel them. It was time to open the black box and satisfy his curiosity. So he slowly opened it. Under the moonlight, he saw the skin of a deer in front of him, which was tangled and gathered like a rolling tape, wrapped around a piece of cloth and prevented it from opening. This was the first time in years that he had felt strength and left his weakness. Sometimes his body temperature rose so high that he became so feverish that he could not move for a while each time he returned to the village. But this time, his weak body was so strong that he had the ability to bring the achievement to the village with pride and promptness. Although he was unaware of its effects. But what mattered most to him was the good feeling that had taken over his whole being.

Encouraged by the sounds he heard, he tore off the piece of cloth and opened the scroll bar, which was wrapped like a letter around a cylinder. Surprisingly, he saw signs and symptoms that shone in the moonlight, as if they contained a message that invites him to read it and understand its contents. At first, confident that he could not understand the messages, he wrapped them again in cylinders and tried to put them inside the box. When he carefully closed the box, he heard voices that intensified, and this time in the midst of a commotion, a louder voice ordered him to take the signs again in front of the moonlight. He was more like a puppet that performed whatever he felt, and as if he had no choice, he immediately opened it and held it in front of the moonlight. His eyes flashed and created a strange feeling in him. This was the first time he thought he knew why he had come there, and he knew very well why he had sleepwalking for so many years. He touched the signs with his fingertips and was sure that he was experiencing a deep feeling in each of them. He moved towards the village and the tribe, knowing that he already knew his mission. Although he was not sure what to expect after telling this story and showing and reading these signs, he continued on his way with heavy steps that showed a great responsibility.

He arrived at the village. He had lost his strength. He reached the main square. He opened the box again and looked inside to make sure it contained the contents and was relieved that it was safe in the box. The sky was clear. This time, he decided to look at the signs and symbols in the sun and study the details now that he is in the city and in the daytime. Strange stars with parallel lines, and a few dots next to the polygons in the form of cuneiform were located. When his eyes fell on them, he regained his energy, and this time, he concluded that these signs could create magical powers in him, and with their help, he could restore the lost power of the chief of the tribe, who was no longer among them, to himself and his family members. So he needed to test its power. He glanced at a passer-by. He was one of the elders of the tribe who never wanted to talk to him and did not respect him. He looked at the stars inside the leather and looked at the passer-by again. Suddenly, a passer-by came up to him and greeted him and even bowed to him, indicating that he was willing to take a few moments to spend time with him. He looked at him and commanded him to gather the members of the tribe together. He did not think he was so influential, but he tried his luck. At the same time, he continued to wait for a few hours for a glorious crowd from the tribe in the middle of the village and wanted to talk to them. The passer-by bowed and looked respectfully and moved towards the tribe. He did not know how much he could trust the stars he had and the lines that were magically placed side by side. But he knew that they were not ordinary lines and signs but contained a message that made him superior to others and made others obedient. At the same time, he hears voices in his ears that sometimes make him laugh and sometimes motivate him to do something. He thought to himself that in a few hours all the people of the tribe would gather around him and what he really wanted to say and why he had asked the members of the tribe to gather. He was sure that he had been ridiculed and subjugated by special energies and that he would certainly, when everyone had gathered, subconsciously say things that he may not have heard before and that were new to him. With a smile on his face and to increase his magic power, this time he carefully examined the contents of the box, which was in the form of signs and symbols and made sure that he had enough energy in his eyes.

Little by little, he heard the members of the tribe gathering in the village square, and soon, he saw all the members gathered in front of him, impatient and noisy, and they did not know why they had gathered at the invitation of the most ordinary member of the tribe. He raised his head so that everyone could see the energy in his eyes. Suddenly, a deep silence engulfed the entire crowd, transferring a great deal of energy. Inevitably, everyone remained silent and knelt helplessly in front of him, not even knowing why they were doing it. He also opened the box and raised the leather skin containing the signs and symbols and showed them to people and inadvertently believed that he had been giving a speech for some time and called everyone to follow what he had shown.

The reflection of this gathering reached the chief of the tribe, who had been in charge for some time. Anger took over his whole being, because he thought he was ignoring the security of the village and calling others to a kind of riot. He was convinced when he heard that the people of the tribe wanted to visit the neighbouring tribes and inform them of what they had seen and heard. Gradually, what the chief of the tribe guessed happened. The chief of the tribe was a member of a seven-member council that had requested an investigation into him. But the passage of time and promotion made him no longer important and did not feel the need for further research. But now, he saw that the situation was moving in the direction that the arrow of the people's gatherings was aimed at him, and that he would be one of the future victims. The subject of the magic box was so colourful that the people of the neighbouring tribes also talked about it, and anyone who did not take it seriously would find himself subconsciously confronted with the energies that frightened him, and like a child from the beginning believed in the signs inside the box.

***

This was the third time in a row that there had been a war between those who believed in the magic black box and those from the tribe who were elders and officials who opposed these superstitions. A bloody and great war in which even other tribes participated. The quarrel had lasted so long that the signs inside the box came to their aid again, causing the other wars to end in his absolute victory, and he soon became an absolute power stronger than the former tribal chief who was one of his relations. The number of his fans and the magic box was increasing day by day until the news of the emergence of a power filled the whole jungle that even others saw themselves as one of his followers. Soon after the tribes in the jungle, the other tribes of the other jungles also considered themselves as his followers, and as this number increased, the sound of singing filled his whole mind, and this was the same song that he had heard the first night after finding the magic box. Other circumstances showed that his journey into the heart of darkness was certainly expedient, and that he had attained this great magical power with the help of special energies, so that anyone could look at those signs and symbols and experience the same power, though less than him. Little by little, the ceremony of honouring the box became popular among the people of the tribes, and every day, they brought the symbolic boxes they had provided in their huts and tents in front of them and put something like the signs and symbols of the magic box in it. After looking at and touching the signs, they got to work. But what surprised everyone was that they felt empowered after the ceremony, even though it was not comparable to his power. But it caused them to do things that were sometimes not common among the people of the tribes and were considered abnormal. But the power of the box was so unpredictable that no one said a word, and they preferred everyone to show their commitment to it to save them from its consequences.

***

The magic box was passed down among the tribal people for several generations, and each of them added a ceremony to honour it. This ceremony was performed every day of the year with special complexities and many people dedicated themselves to it and were considered the custodians of this ceremony. A long time passed and everyone spoke and wrote about what happened that day according to what they had heard. But what has always been a tradition among them was the level of violence that each one took to prove that he was more attached to the black magic box, and that many people were sometimes killed. On the other hand, the whispers and laughter that were heard in the darkness of that night in the jungle were heard every day among the people of the tribes who were already performing as their daily rituals.

Gaurdian of the Castle

Guardian of the Castle

Silence filled the hall. The gaze was on the main entrance of the hall so that the Guardian of the Castle would be present during the planned ceremonies and sit on his chair as the new Guardian of the Castle, which was considered the highest possible position of the city. A special event that had attracted the attention of all the people of the city and promised them that they would have a great change ahead and see him as a saviour who would sacrifice himself to free them from the clutches of evil. A dream that could be fulfilled in the presence of the Guardian of the Castle, and he had the ability to be their saviour and promising the time which is not far away. The people of the city during these years were always waiting for someone to be able to become the hero of the castle and raise his flag to do justice to them. Everything they had been waiting for had arrived, and now they had the footsteps of the guardian in front of their eyes, which was moving slowly and calmly towards the place.

He was accompanied by a delegation of council members who had elected him a few days earlier. A choice that resulted after a week of struggle. At first, it seemed that the council members may have been a little hasty in electing him, and this whisper was occasionally exchanged among the people of the city. Some feared that he was young so that he might not have the necessary experience in managing the castle, and some did not consider him worthy enough to penetrate to such an extent without having the necessary background and introduce himself as one of the elected castles. Some also thought that perhaps a person would be elected who could deal with the prevailing controversy with a strong will or be considered a better known person for the purpose. Even his election as such was one of the most mysterious issues that many people still could not digest. However, even this point could be considered as a factor that doubled the suspicion among the people.

At first, the members of the council had come to the conclusion that they were in a sensitive and special situation in electing the Guardian of the Castle, and perhaps the critical situation had caused them to accept this election. In fact, it felt that perhaps the competition between the two deserving candidates was so close that, in order to avoid a new crisis, they found themselves reaching out to someone who had never been or was so knowledgeable among the council members and he seemed so weak that members can manage him whenever they want. This was the most important factor that accelerated and facilitated the election of the young man. In fact, he was never considered a special option and was only attracted by the council when its members concluded that perhaps the election of a temporary guardian for the castle could alleviate existing external pressures and internal disputes, and this was exactly the ideal situation which was visible to the weakest member of the council, and his youth alone helped them do so. It was enough to temporarily elect him and wait to elect a suitable person for that position at an effective time. But during this period, all matters must be done under the supervision of the council. The only thing was that the council would hold a special show to calm the people so that they would know that no problem threatens them and that the castle will not be left without a guardian.

The people still stared in silence at the presence of the new guardian. The young man, accompanied by a number of companions and entourage, followed him into the foyer, and this was part of a ceremony in which all the castle staff joined hands over the past few days to portray the glory of the guardian. The path from the foyer to the castle guard's chair was covered with a red carpet, and along this path, beautiful flowers came to decorate it. A large crowd of locals, who had been selected to oversee the castle, stood in considerable order on either side of the red carpet, greeted the Guardian of the Castle by holding coloured flowers and waving them to convey the message of the rest of the town and ask him to respond to their joy and happiness on this glorious day. On the other side, in a special place, stood the members of the council who had elected him for this purpose, and with their presence, in addition to welcoming him, they carried a message of support for him. In any case, they had to move the situation forward so that people would not feel worried. They debated for hours about whether people needed to know that the present guardian was only for a certain period of time, and it made no sense to mention it anymore.

For this reason, the seven-member council had kept the matter a secret and intended to select a worthy guardian in a more relaxed manner after the ceremony and after a short period of time had elapsed. To this end, even the chairman of the council took on the responsibility of monitoring and controlling the behaviour, orders and speeches of the interim guardian from moment to moment. In one corner, a select staff of the castle, standing on behalf of others in uniform, stood and waited to see the city's highest official up close and to know under whom they will obey from now on. The special place was also decorated in the best possible way, and it was covered with colourful and fragrant flowers and the chair was placed in a special place, which had given it a kind of sanctity and subconsciously creates the impression in everyone that the Guardian of the Castle cannot be a simple person. And, of course, now that he has been elected, he must have had certain characteristics that have been able to persuade the members of the council to consider him for this position, although there was much opposition. This was all the concerns that basically all the people of the city had in mind and hoped that he would be the person they had been waiting for. Perhaps this was the reason for his uniqueness, because without any background he saw himself on the verge of entering a position where, after sitting on it, he could control and manage all the affairs of the city. The sanctity of the special place had multiplied when he was placed at the highest point of the foyer, and to reach it, he had to climb a few steps and sit in a chair surrounded by dreadful statues. Baskets full of sweets and fruit were also provided for the reception, and these luxuries all showed the importance of this ceremony. The young man's steps were taken so slowly that his splendour was clearly visible. In a special dress and with a strange covering that was more like a uniform, he walked in such a way that his black cape danced beautifully behind his back and the other companions coordinated their movement speed with him in a special coordination so that a good display of order would prevail. At the end of the black cape were embossed gold-coloured patterns in which the black background was clearly visible. The young man stood tall and straight, without even looking around, staring straight at the special place and following the red carpet without a smile, as if he knew exactly what he was going for. This worried the seven-member delegation a little. At the same time, a slow hymn began to play in the foyer, and quickly, the attendees began to sing, which was more like a whisper being uttered, and nothing but a vague melody could be heard. Attendees were simultaneously waving flowers in their hands, creating a magnificent image. His companions followed him without any further movement and did not even look around. It seemed that this different presence of the Guardian of the Castle was a sign of his election, and soon all the doubts and worries of the people were forgotten and they became sure that he was the saviour who was going to save them from that failed situation, and even it was also thought that his youth was a gift that could see him in the chair of the castle for many years.

Amidst the gaze of the audience, the young man found himself in front of a chair, and after a moment's hesitation, sat down slowly on it, looking at the observers. Suddenly, the sound of commotion and joy filled the hall. There was a strange fervour among the people. The young man who until a few days ago saw himself in the council among others, now looks like a saint who was supposed to make people's dreams come true. In fact, even he himself could not believe that the result of the council would affect his life in such a way that he was now called the highest person in the city and called the Guardian of the Castle. But after seeing their welcome in front of him and when he leaned on the guardian's chair, he felt that perhaps there was no one more worthy than him, and that he was in fact the people's choice, and that the divine forces were fully involved in his election. Meanwhile, one by one, the castle staff came and bowed to him, thus confirming his presence in the new position and showing their readiness to perform any service. Then the chairman of the council came to the stage with a wooden tray on which was a small golden sceptre, and without looking at anyone, he walked slowly and confidently to the stand. Silence was restored, and everyone waited for the sceptre to be handed over to its owner. This sceptre is passed from one guardian to the next, and as long as the guardian holds it, he can take the holy forces under his command.

The chairman of the council reached the special place and, as if bowing, picked up his sceptre from the tray and took it to the guardian. He also looked at the sceptre with great respect for a moment and took it from the chairman of the council. He stared at it for a moment and waited for the chairman of the council to leave. At that moment, the excitement of the crowd in the foyer filled the air. Enthusiasm was evident on their faces. But the guardian did not take his eyes off the sceptre for a moment and showed indifference to the emotions of the people.

Significant glances were exchanged between council members that if one paid close attention to them one could easily read their anxiety on their faces. It felt like everything might not go according to plan, and that could jeopardise all of their plans. Maybe they made a hasty choice or it was better to elect one of the two selected people. It was as if they saw themselves as victims of an old rivalry among the council members, and there was no way to see and examine the new behaviour of the temporary Guardian of the Castle. Suddenly, the guardian got up and raised his sceptre as a sign of power, and as the first words heard from him, he called everyone to silence. Everyone fell silent, and a deeper silence spread from the beginning. He then addressed the crowd with words and said: "As the new Guardian of the Castle, I promise you, the people of the city, that as long as you move in the shadow of the castle, you will not be harmed at all and its new guardian will support you forever and does not allow this position to be easily or accidentally changed, or to be a toy in the hands of this or that. Because the new guardian is your elected one and elected by the divine forces, and he will not allow anyone or anything to threaten the position of the permanent Guardian of the Castle." The sound of shouts of joy echoed everywhere. The people of the city were excited and together they shouted in unison to the Guardian of the Castle and addressed him as a saviour.

Then he turned to the council and pointed his sceptre at them and called them one by one. Completely confused, they came to him and, in order to show the situation in their favour, stood up and bowed before the Guardian of the Castle and showed their readiness to serve the castle and its new guardian. It was as if they had forgotten what a decision they had made.

Black Monster

Black Monster

He ran with great speed and excitement, trying to find his way through the dense and crowded trees without looking back. The darkness of the night had greatly frightened him, and he only hoped to get out of the restricted area and out of the forest as soon as possible. The branches of the trees played like a whip on his face, and he could feel the burning and cold air up to his bones. The humidity caused the surface under his feet to slip, and he lost his balance several times while fleeing and fell to the ground. But each time, he got up faster and was completely oblivious to the injuries he sustained. He was covered in mud and was thinking of only one thing that could save his life. Maybe it was better to think more about the consequences before doing so. But he was so determined that he saw himself as a hero who wanted to save the city. But now, everything was different. The hero of the hours ago was only thinking of saving himself and wanted to get to his hut. The sound of his breath coming out of his mouth quickly and briefly seemed so frightening that it added to his fear and panic. He could not even close his mouth for a moment and swallow his saliva. In fact, he felt so dry in his airway that even a thick fog in the middle of the night could not reduce his dryness. It was as if everything was over for him. In those inflammatory moments when he was in a hurry, he thought that he had not chosen the right time to do so. The feeling of suffocation was added to his unfavourable moods and conditions. Although he did not have the opportunity to look back and did not even dare to do so, he knew with all his being that the Black Monster was chasing him, and it would not give up until he was punished for his actions. He does not lift his head. How could he have done so simply and done what he knew was the end of it? In the past few years, there have been those who set foot in the restricted area and did not survive. Some of them were lost forever, and several had found their bodies, each of whom had died strangely. He never wanted to suffer the same fate as a few people before.

His frustration increased every moment, and he inadvertently realised that tears were flowing from his eyes and that the hatred he had in his throat had now caused him to suffocate. He never liked to be a victim and see himself as a corpse that people gathered around him the next morning and regretted. It was enough that he did not just take his adventure seriously and did not take such a big risk. He felt that perhaps before the Black Monster followed him, he did not have a proper understanding of the danger and fear that this would create for him. Perhaps if he had only understood a few percent of this horror, he would never have made such a decision. The moment came to his mind that even if he could cross the forest and get home, he would still not be safe. The illusion of this bothered him while he was running and reduced his motivation to run away. He had entered exactly the current that would defeat him in any case. Either he would be torn to pieces by the Black Monster tonight, or he would die of fear and delusion. But he still ran instinctively and tried to escape. Although he had gradually come to the conclusion that he would be a victim in the end and that no one would even mention him as a hero. It does not matter, however, what others think of him. This kind of thinking is important for people when they are in safe and comfortable and are looking for unattainable titles. But when they are informed, they think that they are in fact losers who have entered into such cases and become victims. Certainly, if time went back and he saw himself in the town square among his other friends talking about a restricted place yesterday, he would no longer show such courage and would not volunteer to reveal the secrets of the restricted place. Something they had talked about many times in their friendly community and even reviewed the dangers over and over again. The victims were all scared to death before death came to them. A young man who found him in the middle of a swamp and another who was torn apart by animals. After their bodies were found, it had all been proven that they had died of fear and death before they plunged into a swamp or were baited by animals or dismembered by a Black Monster. What made him determined was that if doctors confirmed that all the victims had died of fear before being trapped, then he could, because of his courage, overcome his fear and be saved. Something that now shakes his heart with all his being and calls him to death. For a moment, he emptied under his feet and quickly fell to the ground. This time, he seemed to like the incident and was happy that he had accidentally fallen to the ground and had a chance to rest for a moment, without thinking about the monster approaching, but that happiness was shorter than giving him self-confidence or give strength to regain his lost strength. As he struggled to free himself from the mud of the forest, fear again moved him. He hears the roar of the monster, which follows him, and his black shadow moves among the bare winter trees. He got up again and with a little hesitation estimated his distance to the end of the way. It was thought that if he could endure a few more minutes, the slippery and dangerous forest trail would end and reach the main road. However, the main road itself was completely deserted, and at this time of night, nothing but danger awaited him. A bitter smile settled on his face as he recounted in his mind how authoritatively he had told them that he would go to the restricted area alone tonight. Even if he was saved, how could he prove to his friends how far he had come and how he had fought to save himself from the Black Monster. He was sure that they did not believe, and his attempt to do so was in vain. There was only one thing he could prove to his friends, how daring he was to set foot there, and it was precisely his death that made everyone realise that he really did, because the Black Monster is only looking for those who they passed through the dense forest and reached the restricted area. All the victims were all people who risked their lives to dream and arrived in the area at the time of the ban, which was announced in the city. It was announced in the city that no one would enter the forest after nine o'clock at night and go to that area. But he had made his decision, and he wanted to at least prove to himself that the reason for being abandoned there was something other than a Black Monster. It has been said again and again that the Black Monster, with its supernatural powers, has no leniency in taking revenge on other people who do not cooperate with it and will not rest until it takes the life of its victim. The Black Monster does not even allow the morning to come and the fugitive can give news and reports of his condition to others. He, too, had met with exactly the same fate now and knew that there was no escape. When he remembered his friend telling him anxiously that the restricted area was where the Black Monster lived, he regretted how easily he had ridiculed him and seen himself as a knight capable of resisting any creature. He had all the equipment he needed last night and got there. A lantern with a knife and a hunting rifle and suitable clothing that will both keep him warm and not slow him down when necessary. He knew very well how to protect himself from wild animals, because in fact he was also a skilled hunter who hunted at special times for fun. But the Black Monster was not a wild animal. It was more than he could have imagined. He could feel the redness of his blood flowing from the monster's mouth, which made his legs weaker and weaker. Although no one but the victims had seen it, they all had a good picture of the Black Monster in their minds, and they all had something in common. But he had not seen the monster. He had only approached the restricted area and did not even have a chance to see it well. The only thing he remembered about the area was that he saw a cemetery of trees in front of him that had been brutally crushed. Maybe this picture for a few seconds was full of errors, and maybe what he saw was completely different from what he was thinking now. Behind that area, too, he remembered the barbed wire that prevented him from advancing, doubling his hesitation in approaching them. Behind the barbed wire, there was a terrible sound that from time to time was accompanied by something like a tree falling, and a light that increased and decreased the shadow of the monster on the trees. It was all the image that remained in his mind from that moment on. So maybe the monster will have mercy on him and stop chasing him. But that was not the problem. He knew that no mistake was more important to him than crossing the monster's red line. In any case, he had set foot in a place where if he did not see the monster's reaction or was overcome by fear, he would go ahead and discover its secrets. But now, everything was different. He dropped his shotgun and hunting knife on the ground and was fleeing only with speed. What always bothered him was that the hunter wanted to escape, but now, he was fleeing and that no longer bothered him. He had felt the true meaning of fear and could even feel that he was ready to die like everyone else and that his feet were just instinctively moving him forward. He wishes he had told his friends to wait for him on the main road. There was nothing more painful than that he was a victim without any information. All he had in mind was that the Black Monster was building vast areas for its life, and sooner or later, it would take over the entire forest and reach out to the citizens. He felt the wild nature of the monster and knew that no one could stop it. But it was too late for him, and that was when he hurried through the woods and did not even look back to see the monster. He thought that if he came back and saw the monster for a moment, he would lose his motivation to continue and escape, but these contradictory feelings were so loud in him that he was no longer like an ordinary person, and the illusion took over all his mental settings. He was confused, and this caused him to find himself for the second time in a path from which he had passed quickly, and to conclude that he was trapped in a thick fog among the thick trees, and that his estimate was incorrect. His heart ached. He said to himself that it might be better to stand and even turn around and embrace the Black Monster with death, but he did not want to be torn to pieces. Whatever it was, he was free to choose the type of his death. This was the least he could do for himself. He even thought for a moment that he wanted his body to be in good condition in the yard of his cottage and that other citizens should prepare a glorious ceremony for him and bury him in the city cemetery. This was the least he wanted and motivated him to keep trying. Now he no longer thought of saving himself, and what mattered to him was his body, which did not want to be bitten by other creatures. So even to reach this goal, he had to go through the trees and reach the main road. He seemed to have run for a long time and could not continue. He could have slept in his warm bed now, and he regretted how he had risked his life and carelessly thought that his body was safe. Little by little, he smelled death and found himself on the verge of great incident. It happens to everyone but with the difference that he himself chose it and his behaviour was considered a kind of suicide. He should have thought about the fact that others thought he was stupid for doing that.

He could hear the voices of the people who gathered next to his body the next morning and talked about him. There was no applause or excitement in the background, and he could feel how stupidly they stared at his stupidity. This time, he chose a new path in the foggy weather. It was the last chance he had. He knew that he could no longer escape the destiny he had created and found himself gradually surrendering. As he ran, he heard the sound of its footsteps encouraging him to stand. He made his last effort. The voice of the Black Monster was getting closer to him every moment. He even thought that he could feel its shadow in the darkness that overshadowed him. He found himself in disbelief on the main road. As if motivated, he took a moment to look at the foggy trees, and with an incredible leap, set off. Although a kind of joy had taken over his existence, he still found himself trapped by a monster. He recognised the sound of laughter well, and this sound did not leave him a moment. If he was only a little lucky, his situation would not be like this. He wishes he had never left his hut yesterday and not seen his old friends in the town square who now want to run away to prove such things. His friends were definitely adventurous too, but this was not an adventure, it was pure stupidity, because none of his friends even agreed to follow with him. They believed that following him was a great sin that the Black Monster was unlikely to forgive and seek revenge. This part of the route was smoother for him. There was no more news of the withered branches of the trees scratching his whole face and hands, and he could feel the drops of blood flowing down his lips, making the smell of death more visible to him. He raised his hand helplessly and wiped the sweat from his forehead to soften the cold that hit his face a little and reduce the chills in his body. It was not far from the main road to his hut. He knew he would get there soon. Gradually, his sense of hope grew stronger again, but the monster's voice made that hope dry in his heart. He now believed in monsters. He remembered a few people in the city who said that there was no monster and that everything was born of fantasy, or maybe it was a rumour or an illusion that was common among everyone, but if he had the opportunity, he would have seen one of the citizens just before his death, he would tell him that the nature of the monster was real and that he felt it with all his heart. He no longer wanted to let go of the cold morning breeze to get rid of these thoughts. Now, like other citizens, he realised the existence of the monster and accepted that the Black Monster intended to destroy the people and take over the entire forest. But why didn't the mayor and others want to get rid of the monster with the help of the people? Perhaps they made the best decision and instead of sacrificing others, they only warned and persuaded the people that this is a law and no one has the right to go to a restricted area for any reason, and if someone survives from there, he will definitely face the law. In their view, no citizen should make arbitrary decisions and risk his own life and the lives of others, an enemy that was far more terrifying than the Black Monster, and it killed them. He had now concluded that he had seen the monster, but he was not sure that the other victims had reached the same conclusion and stage with him. He was out of breath and in no hurry to get to his hut. He felt very close to the end of his work. He hesitated for a moment, stood up, put his hand on his knee and bent down to take a rest. A terrible voice came closer to him. He stood up again and began to walk fast until he found himself on the threshold of the city. A city that now looked like a city of the dead and looked deserted. All the citizens respected the rules and stayed at home before nine o'clock so that the Black Monster would not come to them. He felt a new life again and opened the door of the hut, closing it behind him as fast as he could and pushing the table towards it so that the door would not open. He looked for a lantern to light it in the dark. The anxiety was so great that he could not light the lantern. Suddenly, he heard a doorbell. The Black Monster had gotten there. The door was knocking as hard as it could. He was not really sure if he was right or illusory, but his inner feelings were full of fear and panic. He hurried to the stairs and climbed up. Several times, with the sound of knocks on the door, his foot slipped and hit the edges of the stairs. But his nervous system was paralysed and he no longer felt pain. He found himself on the verge of something. He went to his bedroom and locked himself there. He heard a terrible sound that it was able to break through the entrance and enter the hut. He can even hear his footsteps stepping firmly on the wooden stairs. He shouted in fear. During this time, he did not have time to shout and ask for help. On ordinary days, he hears the conversations of his neighbours in the nearby huts, but it is as if they are all deaf tonight and do not hear his screams. He continued until he made sure the Black Monster had reached the back of the bedroom. He slowly stepped back and entered the balcony overlooking his bedroom. He could hear the door shaking, which was still crumbling. He tried to concentrate and convince himself that maybe all these events and the Black Monster were just his imaginations that were alive and moving. But his heart rate was so high that he was out of breath. He leaned back a little and leaned unconsciously on the balcony railings. The monster's roar grew louder, and he could see the shadow, as it entered the room. He paused for a moment and calmed his broken breath. He felt dizzy and was on the verge of falling. The next morning, city security forces surrounded his house, and people gathered above his body, which had fallen from the balcony. Everyone talks about him and the cause of his death.

Some believed that he had died as a result of carelessness, and some considered the cause of his death to be distress. Some of his friends were also talking to the police, announcing yesterday and his decision to go to the restricted area and shaking their heads in regret. At that moment, the mayor arrived and went over his body and quickly asked the doctor about the cause of death. The doctor also turned over his notes, stating that the cause of his death was fear, which caused him to fall from the balcony. The mayor, meanwhile, turned to the crowd and said loudly, "This is the fate of those who ignore the warnings and enter the restricted areas. The Black Monster took the life of another of our citizens. It does not want anyone to enter its territory. Stay away from there so that we do not see such things happening."

Empty Frame

Empty Frame[*]

He entered the Hall of Mirrors and, as always, found himself in front of mirrors that surrounded him around the hall and reflected the image of him from every angle. Each image was immersed in another and continued in a continuous line, and with the slightest movement, he could see countless images that moved and represented him like a large army. The mirrors were each arranged at appropriate angles with a special elegance, and the floor of the hall was covered with a

---

[*]*In psychiatry, extreme narcissism, based on psychological and personality traits, is identified in excessive love with unbridled narcissism and is considered a kind of mental disorder. Narcissism is derived from the Greek word for narcissus (Narges, the myth of Narcissus). Narcissus, or Narges, was a good-looking young man who shunned love of Echo and was condemned to fall in love with the image of his face in a pool of water. The name Narges flower is derived from this legend. When Narcissus does not reach his love (his reflected face), he sits on the fountain so sadly that it turns into a flower.*

white stone. Surely, the design of such a hall took many years so that he could easily step into it and see his awe in it. The mirror work was done so artistically that it easily attracted everyone's attention, and on the other hand, it gave a hundredfold beauty to its audience. A high ceiling that made him taller and a lighting that gave him a special effect from all sides. He stepped forward and monitored his reflection in the mirrors. It was definitely he who gave meaning to the Hall of Mirrors and multiplied its architectural art. He went to one of the mirrors and stood in front of it, staring at himself carefully. The fit and the beauty were so tangled with the charm that he quickly forgot about the Hall of Mirrors and was fascinated by his image. But he was not just fascinated by his image. Something beyond that called him from within and put heat on his forehead, the red of which was visible in the mirror in front of him. He found himself happier than any creature that had all the attractions, and he knew that his responsibility was beyond what he had. He could not act like everyone else and ignore all his unique characteristics. It seemed that it was worthless to ignore all his outward and inward talents and abilities that could lead him to the lowest possible level. He was happy to realise his perfection and to feel his specialness with all his being. This awareness was also a sign of his rich intelligence that distinguished him from others, although others envied his condition and called him isolated. But it was different. To be among the common people or to walk in the Hall of Mirrors, right where not everyone has access to and enjoy the reflection of his image. He certainly chose to be alone and was satisfied with that choice. Maybe if he was like everyone else, he would not consider himself worthy of the

Hall of Mirrors. But now, his destiny is moving in a direction that many people have been deprived of, and this has put a smile on his face. Hanging between the mirrors, paintings or photographs and pictures of his profile were enough to make him more special and attractive. He believed that he was inherently superior to others and should keep his distance from them so that their populist circumstances would not tarnish his glorious attire, A garment that was carefully sewn by the most skilful tailors and made of the finest fabrics and created the conditions appropriate to what he was wearing. He was so fascinated by his image that no other beauty could satisfy him. From his point of view, it was concluded that not everyone deserves so much attention from the Creator, and if he has such an opportunity, then he should appreciate it and keep himself away from pollution and not let any human being approach him without knowing his true existence and interacting with him. He got closer to the mirror again. He could see his eyes shining like a diamond, and there was a sense of satisfaction in them. There was only one thing that always bothered him, and that was the reflection of a voice that was always twisting in the hall and rioting in it with its waves. He had tried many times to find the source of the sound reflection, but so far, he had not succeeded. He walked into the middle of the hall, watching his profile up and down for the last time, then spun around and came out of the small door in the corner of the hall. This led him to his office. It was definitely necessary for him to walk through the Hall of Mirrors every day before stepping into his office to remind him of his perfection and to inform him of his true worth, and he would certainly spend more time in the Hall of Mirrors if the reflection of the sound did not resonate in his ear. He felt so happy in the Hall of Mirrors that he never wanted to leave. This feeling was not a small matter. In fact, it was this feeling that shaped his character and made his office strangely special and beautiful. He looked around and went to his desk and sat on it with authority. Everything was in place, and he saw order as the source of the gift he possessed, and it was so important for him, because if there were no order, his specialness would be lost among all others, and he could not display a true picture of what actually he is. It was a great success. There were the best accessories and the highest quality facilities on his desk, and he placed a photo frame in a corner of it, which changed the photo inside every day. Every morning before coming to his office, he brought a picture of himself to decorate his desk. He carefully placed it in the frame on the table and carefully placed the previous image in his bag to use again. This was his most important program every day. Next to the photo frame were small mirrors with precise angles that he could see in any way he leaned on the chair so that he would not forget for a moment and would not doubt the extent of his charm and abilities. He raised his head and, as if trying to get some strength from somewhere, looked at the painting on the wall, thinking that it would be better to change his picture on the wall from time to time, which gave his office a look. He then picked up the pen on the table, obsessively opened it, put the tip on a piece of paper and began writing, as if to give an important order. After a moment, he wrote the last line and folded the paper carefully, then placed his hand on the bell next to the table and pressed it to call his secretary. In fact, his only connection to the outside world was that of his secretary, who, at the sound of a bell, opened his office door and hurried into the room to communicate the orders issued to others or to report on the orders previously issued. But this time, it did not happen. If he did not hear the bell, he knew the cause was malfunction. He tried again so that he might both call the secretary and act as a warning to make him more responsible for the task at hand. But still, nothing happened. He got up thinking that the secretary might be in trouble or bored and absent today. But he soon responded to the thought that the secretary had always informed him, and that this was unprecedented. So it could be a more important and serious issue than he thought. It took a while. He went to the window and looked at the people from the top floor of the building. They were moving and sometimes passing each other slowly and sometimes quickly. Sometimes they stood and talked and sometimes they were indifferent and did not pay attention. Their faces, though not very visible from this distance, could easily feel normal. A young man and woman walking together, or an old man walking and a little girl selling bouquets into his hand. Really, why and with what motivation did they continue and what future awaited them? He could not even bear the ordinary moments of their being, let alone live like them and continue without any tomorrow. He returned immediately so as not to witness such anomalies and to close his eyes to see the beauties on which he was created and to understand them well in himself. At that moment, the reflection of the voice came to him again. It was the only thing that bothered him. He put his hands on his forehead and pressed it. If he could only find the sound source, he would have no problem. He went to the bell and rang it again. But still, his secretary was not accountable. He felt a little uneasy. It was as if he had not started his day the way he wanted. He felt that while the servant was not accountable, he could not step into the outside world. He closed the communication channels to himself and thought that he was left alone in his office, which was the size of a hall and had no way out. On the one hand, the reflection of the voice bothered him, and on the other hand, the absence of the secretary. At times when the secretary could not come to work, someone else was replaced, and now that he was not present at work without notice, he did not know what to do. He walked the length and width of the room a little anxiously so that he might find a way out. He had never encountered such a problem. He looked at the door for a moment and soon tried to forget what he was thinking. He could not open the door and easily find himself among employees or ordinary people. He heard the reflection of sound in his ears again. The same voice that kept him away from his true self. He was confused. He held his head in his hands. He thought it would be better to go back to the glass room and close that day. But again, the reflection of the voice in his mind called him to himself. He immediately went to his desk and picked up the mirror, looked at it as if he wanted to regain his energy and clear his doubts and make sure that he was special and very quickly regained his sense of calm. But if the servant did not come for the next few days or had a problem, how could he save himself from the captivity he had felt it for the first time? He felt the reflection of the sound again. He was a little careful. The reflection came from outside the room. He walked slowly and confidently towards it and stood in front of the door. He thought for a moment that now that the secretary had not arrived, it would be better to look for the main source of sound reflection in order to solve the problem for himself once and for all and restore calm forever. With that thought, he saw his hand on the handle in the room that was spinning. He felt that he had exercised a great deal of courage, and that if he were among ordinary people, he might become infected and his charms and abilities would be damaged. Doubtful, his curiosity led him to open the door and connect with the outside world. He saw himself to open the door. Everyone was moving and no one was paying attention to him. On the one hand, he felt that he had been insulted, and on the other hand, he was happy that he was not being paid attention to, and that he was able to look for the source of sound reflection away from the eyes of others. The sound was louder than ever. He found himself at the end of a corridor that ended in an elevator, pulling him towards it like a magnet. He went inside the elevator. There was a full-length mirror in front of him. He turned his head and did not look in the mirror for the first time. After a while, he opened the elevator, and this time, he was standing in the middle of the same street that he had been watching a few minutes before. He did not like the way people came and went, but he tried to ignore it. He stepped in the direction the voice was calling him. After a few moments, he stood in front of a little girl who was selling the same beautiful bouquets of daffodils. The girl looked at him and immediately handed him the bouquet with a smile. He refused but suddenly realised that the sound was reflected through the daffodils, which now intoxicated him with its perfume. He took the bouquets from her and carried them to her face and sniffed them. He was intoxicated. He was happy to find the source of the reflection and wanted to pay for it, but he remembered that he had not brought his wallet with him. He removed the bouquet to explain to the girl or to ask her to meditate and allow him to go to the office and pay for it. But he realised with complete disbelief that no one was in front of him, and if he did not have a bouquet in his hands, he believed that he had definitely a dream and that the reflection of his voice had disturbed him. He looked around. He did not see the girl except the comings and goings of the others. He imagined the innocent face of the girl. He felt that he knew her and that the girl was pursuing a goal. His face was so fiery. The picture of the girl was the same person whom the Hall of Mirrors had warned and prevented from approaching years ago. The failed love and the hall that had isolated him and now people were moving together and he was left alone in the street with a bouquet of daffodils. A young couple approached him. The man had mistaken him for a florist and asked him to sell a bouquet of flowers to present to his love. He came to himself suddenly. There were tears in his eyes when he saw them. He remembered his past. He cut the flower branch and gave it to them, and after that, he would give the flower branch to any couple who passed in front of him, and he would enjoy it. He took the last branch of the flower in his hand and returned to his room. Along the way, he saw other employees staring at him in surprise. Employees who had not seen him until a few minutes ago did not take their eyes off him. He went to his office. He left the door open. He filled his glass with a bottle of water and put a daffodil branch in it. He removed the photo frame from the table and pulled out the photo inside it and placed the empty frame next to the daffodil branch. Meanwhile, he slowly pushed his desk towards the Hall of Mirrors, blocked it and decided never to go to the Hall of Mirrors again.

Lottery Tickets

Lottery Tickets

"You are the winner of one million. Congratulations! Surely, there are many who would like to be in your place now. You can go to our office tomorrow morning with your lottery ticket in hand and receive the desired amount, and of course, I must add that you are very lucky. Congratulations again and see you tomorrow."

It was unbelievable at all. He was standing still, staring at the ticket in his hand. The phone was in his hand and he did not know what to answer. In fact, even if he knew, he would not be able to say anything. He checked the numbers on the ticket several times with the secretary who called. There was no room for doubt. At first, he thought it might be a continuation of the joke he had with his best friend yesterday in the last hours of the lottery. He thought to himself that this was another of his amusing behaviours and simply played him. But the seriousness of the secretary and the phone number he called were the same as the phone numbers on the ticket, proving exactly that there was no joke and that the matter was quite serious, and instead of being surprised, he should be happy that his name has been chosen as the winner among thousands upon thousands of people. He had gone through a series of successive failures and felt that he deserved a better and more dignified life, and that was why he was named one of the award winners. Something he always believed in and was sure that one day he would go through hard times and get him what he deserved. The continuous beep in his ear warned him to put the phone back in place and think about his future plans. Involuntarily, he took the ticket to his face and kissed it. However, it was a significant amount of money and could have completely changed his situation today and led him to peace and comfort. He could sit for hours and think about his future plans, how he could spend the rest of his life in complete prosperity and even do great things. He needed a pen and paper to plan for the amount he earned in the lottery. It was time to be vigilant and pay attention to all aspects of his work. He no longer wanted to recklessly destroy all the unique opportunities that awaited him. So in a hurry, as if he had little time, he went to the desk, picked up the paper and pen and sat down at the desk. Now he needed to think great and do millions of things. A greater world had to be imagined. But this was the first time he had thought about such a sum. Because of this, he felt a sense of failure and then anxiety. He realised that he could not think like the rich and could not have a specific plan. On the other hand, he was worried about how to protect this amount so that he would not lose it. He first thought that he should change his apartment and move to a place where the conditions were right. But the next moment, he came to the conclusion that he should invest and take up a job and profession and multiply this huge capital, and after raising one million to several million, think of a suitable place to live. However, if he wanted to live in a good place, he had to pay a considerable amount of money for it, which prevented him from running a successful business. But things could have been better if he alone had won the Ten Million Prize instead of the One Million Prize, becoming the first person or at least the third person to win the Three Million Prize. At that time, he no longer had to think about investing and deprive the sweetness of this great opportunity. If only he was the second winner and his prize was three million, he could ignore one million and buy a suitable place and invest for himself with the rest of the money. He felt that even at the peak of happiness, there is always one thing that causes a person to not be able to taste happiness at all. He thought to himself that he was a contented person with no expectation of ten million, but I wish that this could have been more fruitful and saved him from any anxiety. Although this amount was too much for him and he had no purpose to use it, it still made him responsible and made him think. The thought that if he was the first winner, he was excited. He picked up the pen again. He had not yet managed to write anything down. But he knew he had to pay his debts first. However, he could do it with the least amount of money. But he said to himself, now that no one has noticed that I have won, then it is better for me to pay my debts by investing and making a profit in this way and not to touch the original money, lest I spend it bit by bit and have no guarantee for future. Debt payment was also cancelled. Examining every single one of the ideas that came to his mind, he was convinced that he had no choice but to invest and trade. But he did not have the expertise to handle this large sum. On the other hand, he did not trust anyone to achieve his desires through partnership. Demands that were not far from the mind.

It was in these thoughts that he suddenly heard the phone ring again. At first, he thought that maybe he was wrong and that they had called to announce their mistake and that there was no such thing as a One Million Prize. But after reviewing his conversation with the secretary, he recalled that he had been asked several times if there was anything wrong, and that he had said by name and address that he was lucky. He got up and went to the phone. He hesitated to answer, for fear had taken hold of his being. He remembered yesterday, where it all started with a simple joke. In any case, it was not advisable to pick up the phone. On the other hand, the dropped number was not related to the lottery office. But he had to be very careful from now until tomorrow morning so that no one would find out. He had to hide, and for at least a few hours left, he would not show himself to anyone, or it would be better if he left the city for a while tomorrow after receiving the award, and all this came from a joke that made him the luckiest person in town, and ten million or a million did not matter. He had to protect himself from his best friend. Especially if he finds out that the lottery ticket that he jokingly exchanged with him yesterday cost him as much as a million. As usual, they both always had fun and laughter, and that was another part of their fun behaviour. Both laughing exchanged their lottery tickets and told each other that if someone won, they would give the other twenty percent of what they received, and they eagerly went to the counter and changed their personal information. He thought to himself that it was his right to get the money, so there was no need for him to have a guilty conscience or to be afraid of another call. He had not done anything wrong, and he wondered if he could have asked for twenty percent if he had won his lottery ticket. They did not write anything officially and everything was said jokingly. How could he prove that such a promise had been made, and on the other hand, how could he know at all that he had won with his best friend's lottery ticket? In fact, his luck started when they jokingly changed the lottery ticket they had prepared.

He immediately unplugged the phone. It was better not to answer anyone. Even if he is not an old friend. He could not pass this amount for a moment and wanted to keep it as long as he could. He considered this situation his right and did not want to make anyone else his partner for no reason. He even told himself that he might have received a heavenly call that he could exchange tickets with his old friend. In fact, his old friend was in a good financial position and certainly did not need these funds. So why did he have to put himself in trouble to please him? Now that he thought well, they were not compatible in terms of camaraderie and friendship, and this would be a turning point to end this seemingly sincere friendship, which was mostly accompanied by jokes and nasty jokes. In other words, his prestige at this age had degraded with these useless jokes. They did not share the same criteria of friendship from the beginning. So this was a good excuse to end this relationship. He hurried to the lights of his apartment and turned them all off so as not to be considered a threat. It is possible that he may come to his apartment and ask for his share because his friend did not answer the phone. Of course, this feeling was not far from his mind, and it could have been even worse, and he claimed that he had bought the lottery ticket first and that was his right. But they changed all the ownership information in the system that day. So this hypothesis was practically impossible, but if he claimed, it might have caused him trouble. Therefore, it was the condition of reason to be careful and consider all the possibilities so that tomorrow morning, after receiving the money and depositing it in his bank account, he would be safely away from that city for a while so that he would not be considered a threat. He looked at his watch, there was still a long way to go from the night, and the seconds were moving very slowly. If he wanted to put an end to this influx of thoughts and have a better time, he should sleep so that he would not notice the passing of it, and he would arrive at the office at eight o'clock tomorrow and receive the prize before a problem arose. But if his friend had been there since early in the morning, what would he have done and what policy would he have pursued? These were all possibilities that bothered him at every moment. So in the morning, he has to go there anonymously, observing all aspects, and he would not enter the company office until he was sure. But how could his friend know that he was the winner? When someone wins, they only call him and not on anyone else. So this hypothesis was solved for him, and he felt calm and told himself that it is better to sleep on the bed to avoid anxiety and to think about what the rich people of the city do with their money. In any case, this was a good example for him, and he could act like them and, in addition to investing, learn rich behaviours, which he desperately needed.

He arrived at the office at eight o'clock in the morning, and before entering there, checked the situation several times and spent a few minutes in the taxi to be informed from all sides without being seen. But since his nightmares were not unreasonable, he was surprised to see his friend wandering the streets suspiciously, examining the situation. He was right. He was aware. Many people knew him in the lottery company. However, he was an influential person and was definitely informed that the lottery ticket he renamed yesterday has now won one million. He wishes he received this amount without any stories or stress and did not have so much torment of conscience, fear and worry. After a look of confusion, his friend entered the office and now he has to wait in a taxi for him to get out. Fortunately, the ticket was in his hand and no one would be able to receive it without it. The only solution was to wait for him to leave. It took him about a quarter of an hour to see him again rush out of the office and quickly grab a taxi and get on and leave. He could not trust it, perhaps he had entrusted it to the clerk there, so that he could call him immediately after his presence, and he, too, could quickly get there from the side alley. As if he had become part of their show. He pointed to the taxi driver to stand in front of the office and be ready so that he could leave quickly by the time he left the company office, and that a good reward awaited him. However, he could not wait any longer and had to take the risk. So he used all his strength and got out of the taxi and entered the office looking around. He looked around inside the company office. There were three employees working, and he was very careful that no one reached for the phone and informed him. He quickly took the ticket out of his pocket and handed it to the cashier.

He, too, with a smile as if he was overjoyed by his client's happiness, took the ticket and after doing some administrative work and filling out a few forms, brought it to him to sign and receive the money. He looked at the table and at the entrance and the taxi that was waiting for him outside. Everything was under control. The clerk then handed him the final form with the winner's name on it to sign, and he looked at it and signed it, writing his account number in front of his name. Meanwhile, something unusual suddenly caught his attention. He was careful. One of the above names came to him familiar and he was surprised to see the name of his old friend who had won the Ten Million Prize and he had gone there a few minutes ago and received it. And this was exactly what was made possible by his lottery ticket. In a state of shock, he also thought that even if he got twenty percent of that Ten Million Prize, it would be two million, which was actually more than the amount he won. He signed the form and realised that he was still on the path to his usual misfortunes.

The story series "The World Behind Glass" tries to depict a world that every human being creates in his subconscious and lives in fear. A world that is bigger than he imagined and beyond the world in which he lives. Every time he tries to know himself in the world of his imagination, but every moment he finds himself in a labyrinth that brings him back to the beginning of the road and creates eerie and scary conditions for him. Frustration and fear pervade his whole being, and every moment a man reacts differently from what makes up his character.